DATE DUE

MAR 3 0 2000	FE 0 2 '07		
APR 1 7 2000	MR 0 2 '07		
MAY 0 1 2000	OC 0 9 '09		
FEB 2 6 2001	NO 1 7 '11		
MAR 1 1 2002	SE 1 0 '12		
OCT 1 8 2002	SE 2 6 '13		
OCT 3 0 2002	AP 1 1 '16		
DEC 1 6 2002			
FEB 1 9 2003			
OCT 2 7 2003			
DEC 2 2005			
DEC 2 0 2005			
OCT 2 3 2006			
GAYLORD			PRINTED IN U.S.A.

THE
DROWNED

Elizabeth Levy

Hyperion Books for Children
New York

To my editor, Lauri London, who gave me the image that wouldn't leave my mind or heart and who didn't let me rest on my humor. Together we pushed for something deeper and I am so grateful.

And to Elaine Markson—agent and friend for over twenty years—who believed in this book from the beginning.

Text © 1995 by Elizabeth Levy.

Printed in the United States of America.

FIRST EDITION
1 3 5 7 9 10 8 6 4 2

This book is set in 17-point Venetian.

ISBN: 0-7868-0135-2
CIP applied for.

LILY REFUSED TO LOOK AT THE OCEAN. Although she could hear the waves, she wouldn't look at them. She laughed at herself. She had talked her aunt into taking her in for the summer on the beach. She never liked giving in to fear—so if she were afraid of the ocean, it was just like her to insist on living by it for the summer.

She noticed a guy staring at her. He was one of the young men hired to take the tourists in Atlantic City from casino to casino in rolling wicker chairs. She stared back. The boy was incredibly handsome. His face and arms were tanned golden brown, and yet his skin looked almost translucent. His face looked young, but the way he held himself made him look older. He didn't slouch the way most boys did. He was tall and slender. He smiled at her. Her bike made clicking sounds as she rolled along the Boardwalk. She didn't want to stop, but she found herself slowing down as if her bike were on automatic pilot.

Clark watched, grinning to himself, as Lily braked and stepped off her bike. He had wanted her to stop and she had. It was almost too easy. Her looks appealed to him. Her wavy hair was unruly, almost like a child's drawing of a curly-haired witch. There was nothing small or fragile about her. She had a sturdy build. Her legs were muscled, like an athlete's.

Clark looked out at the waves, turning his back on the girl, testing his power. He would let her come to him. He thought of the ocean as his teacher. The ocean was the ultimate thief. Like the ocean, Clark felt it was in his power to take what he wanted. He stretched, getting pleasure from the fact that his muscles ached. It made him feel alive. Every summer began like this, as if some insane coach had chained him to a weight machine for twenty-four hours.

He loved returning to the freedom of the Boardwalk, always had, loved it as much as he loved body surfing in the waves. The Boardwalk and the ocean, the two places where he felt free and alive. And there was always a girl like—Lily, just ripe for the picking. He turned back. She was taking too long. She hadn't walked toward him at all.

Lily had felt herself pulled irresistibly toward the boy with the chair. But then she paused in front of a neon sign advertising Tarot Cards and Palms Read—Lucky Numbers Divined. From inside the shop, the fortune-teller had seen Lily stop her bicycle and hesitate, staring at the young chair pusher. The fortune-teller came outside, dressed in a lilac housecoat and old rubber flip-flops. She pretended that she had come out to water the flowers in front of her shop. "It's a lovely morning, isn't it?" asked the fortune-teller.

Lily nodded. She saw the boy with the rolling chair

continue to gawk at her across the Boardwalk. She gazed back. Even though he was wearing sunglasses, she could tell he was staring at her breasts. She crossed her arms in front of her. Clark hadn't missed the way Lily was hugging herself, and he knew he was the cause of it. He took a step closer.

"Want to come inside?" the fortune-teller asked Lily.

Lily shook her head.

"I could bring you luck," said the fortune-teller. "Everyone wants luck in Atlantic City."

Lily hesitated. She looked at the tourists walking up and down the Boardwalk, carrying plastic cups of quarters. She needed luck as much as any of them.

Just then one of the tourists, an older woman dressed in an electric blue warm-up suit with white piping, tapped Lily on the arm. "Do you know where they crown Miss America?" asked the woman.

The fortune-teller looked angry for a second. Then she smiled at the newcomer. "Why don't you both come inside the shop? I can bring luck to the two of you."

"Can you really divine lucky numbers?" asked the tourist, jiggling her small cup of quarters.

"Certainly," said the fortune-teller.

Clark scowled to himself. First the fortune-teller had interfered with his getting the girl, and now the tourist. He took a step closer. Lily tried to ignore him. She consulted a map that her aunt had given her.

Clark watched her. He wasn't going to let this girl

go. He didn't want to lose her to the tourist or to the fortune-teller. He knew all about fortune-tellers. He had grown up with them, learned from them. Fortune-tellers took money by playing with people's fears. And Clark knew more than most about fear. He knew what it was like to have something as precious as life itself stolen from you.

Clark had no respect for punks who robbed at knifepoint or with a gun. Anybody could get what they wanted that way. It was easy to make someone afraid for his or her life—a knife at the throat, a gun in the belly, who wouldn't give up their money that way? But to steal something from someone without them knowing it, that took skill. Clark stole for the adrenaline rush, the tickle and tease of always knowing he was smiling and being charming only so he could move in, get close and take what he wanted.

"Would you two lovely ladies like a ride?" he said to Lily and the tourist. He lowered his sunglasses and widened his eyes. He had long eyelashes, the kind his mother said were wasted on a boy. His eyes were green, grass green without a fleck of brown in them.

"I think I'll skip the chair," said the tourist. "I like a little exercise. I get stiff after the long bus rides."

Lily noticed the anger that flickered across the boy's face. She felt an overpowering urge to tease him. "I like to walk too," she said lightly. "I just took the bus down last night." She pointed the woman down the Boardwalk toward the convention center. "That's where you'll find the place where they crown

Miss America." The woman hesitated. She looked at her watch. The casinos had reopened for the morning. She turned toward the fantasy blue and green turrets of the casino at the Taj Mahal. Marble elephants guarded the steps. "Maybe I'll just try my luck."

Lily patted the woman on the arm. "Good luck," she said. The woman grinned at her. "What's your name?"

"Lily," answered Lily.

"Mine is June," said the woman. "Lilies and June. We sort of go together, don't we? Maybe you *will* bring me good luck." She waved as she went into the casino.

The fortune-teller gave Lily a disgusted look and went back inside her shop.

Clark put back on his sunglasses. "Thanks for cheating me out of a fare."

Lily frowned. "I didn't cheat anybody."

"You had to go be the cute little guide. 'Oh, the place where they crown Miss America is down the Boardwalk.'" Clark imitated Lily's North Jersey accent perfectly. "Guiding tourists is *my* job. You also cheated the fortune-teller. She thought she had a live one."

Lily looked at the fortune-teller's shop guiltily. "I guess she could put a curse on me."

"Curses are an Atlantic City specialty," Clark said.

"Just my luck." Lily looked at his rolling chair. "Is that your summer job?"

"Yes, a job that takes a lot of skill."

"I'm looking for a job. I'd take anything. Are there girl pushers?"

Clark laughed. "Funny, you don't look like any drug dealer I've ever known."

"That's not what I meant."

Clark grinned. "I know. Actually, there are only a certain number of chairs allowed on the Boardwalk. You've got to have a license, and I've had mine a long time." He flipped his tag. Lily made a face.

"Don't get mad at me. I didn't make up the rules."

Lily shrugged. "I really need to earn money this summer." She perched on the back of a bench with her back to the ocean. The benches on the Boardwalk faced in toward the casinos and not toward the sea. Clark stood next to her, deliberately allowing his elbow to touch hers. He stuck out his right hand. "Clark DeLuge."

Lily took his hand. It felt surprisingly cold, even though the sun was hot. Clark was obviously trying to pick her up, although the word "pickup" had always made her laugh. At 5'9" and 140 pounds of muscle from playing midfield on varsity soccer, no one was going to pick Lily up very easily.

"Lily Potter."

"Lily Potter." Clark repeated her name, licking the edge of his mouth. "I guess you've had to endure a lot of potted plant jokes."

"I've heard them all, thank you."

"Lily's a nice name though. Were lilies your mother's favorite flowers?"

"My father's," answered Lily, immediately sorry that she had. Why couldn't she remember there was no law that she had to answer every question that was asked.

Clark caught something in Lily's voice, a hint of fear when she mentioned her father. The fear pleased him, not just that she was afraid, but that he had been able to pick up on that she was afraid of the ocean. That meant that he was starting the summer with all his antennae working. Every summer he worried that his reactions would be just a split second slower, that his ability to read feelings and fear would have decayed. He studied Lily's face. Hers was an easy face to read.

"You don't have to talk about your father if you don't want to," he said softly.

Lily looked up at him shocked. "Are you a mind reader?" she demanded.

Clark laughed at her. "No," he said.

Lily was uncomfortable. It seemed as if he had read her mind about her father.

Clark looked out at the waves, pausing, waiting to see if Lily would force herself to look at what she feared. She was afraid of the ocean, and she was just a little bit afraid of him, afraid that he already knew her too well. He smiled again, feeling good. The summer was starting just right.

2

LILY HATED SHOWING SHE WAS NERVOUS. She refused to lick her lips or let Clark know that he had gotten under her skin. She felt he was laughing at her, and it made her want to teach him a lesson.

Clark sensed her pulling back. He didn't want the conversation to end so he switched to a more neutral topic. "Did you know when the Boardwalk was first built it had no railing? People used to get drunk and fall off, even kill themselves."

"I suppose I could make money telling little old ladies how to get killed in Atlantic City. After all, my father majored in that."

Clark laughed out loud, but he didn't ask her to explain. Lily was embarrassed. She couldn't imagine what had caused her to blurt out that crack about her father. It wasn't like her. Normally, she didn't talk about her father, especially to strangers. She glanced behind her at the ocean. It was calm, the waves barely rippling onto the sand—more like a big lake than the Atlantic Ocean. The water looked inviting, especially at its edge where it had been warmed by the sun as it lapped the sand. But the ocean's allure didn't tempt her. The restless feeling she had since dawn hadn't really eased. She got off the bench and started to get on her bike. "Wait," said Clark. "Take a walk with me."

Lily hesitated, but she liked the fact that he had felt the urge to ask her. "Okay." She smiled at Clark. She pushed her bike beside him as he pushed his empty chair. They passed more and more people as the day buses from New York City and Philadelphia dropped off their passengers.

"Half these people look bored silly already," said Lily.

"Sometimes I think the old people use the rolling chairs just so they can get us pushers to talk to them."

"Yoo-hoo! Hey Lily!"

Lily turned around. She couldn't imagine who besides her aunt would know her in Atlantic City, and her aunt would still be asleep. It was June, the woman whom she had met in front of the fortune-teller's. In just the few minutes that had passed, the woman had exchanged her small plastic cup for a bucket about the size of a giant tub of popcorn. "Look what I just won!" June shouted, waving at Lily. She showed Lily and Clark her large bucket of quarters. "You *were* lucky for me."

"You know," Clark said, in his most charming voice, "when you win, you're supposed to take a ride on a rolling chair. It's an Atlantic City tradition. All the great gamblers do it. It brings you continued good luck."

June looked dubious. "How much?" she asked.

"Just three dollars for a short ride," said Clark.

"And believe me, you don't want to break tradition. It could mean bad luck." He made it sound a little like a threat.

"I do have to meet my friends at Caesar's Palace." June giggled. She counted out twelve quarters and handed them to Clark. Then she patted the seat beside her. "Come sit with me Lily. It's my treat."

"Will I make it too heavy?" Lily asked Clark.

"Yeah, right," said Clark.

"I'm not exactly a lightweight," Lily said.

"I think I can handle it," said Clark. Lily locked up her bike and took a seat on the chair. The rolling chair had a high curved back, almost like a swan's neck and a cheerful striped fringed awning for shade.

"Isn't this fun, Lily?" June settled back on the cushions. She clutched the giant bucket of quarters in her lap. Her cheeks were flushed. Clark pushed them slowly—no faster than if they were walking. There was something regal about being pushed in the chair. "Do you know where the bedroom is?" June asked. "Someone was telling me about it on the bus."

"Bedroom?" repeated Lily.

"The one where that poor boy drowned?"

"Somebody drowned in a bedroom?" asked Lily. She had visions of an overflowing Jacuzzi. Lily turned around to Clark. "Ever heard of a bedroom where some boy drowned?" she asked.

Clark cupped his hand to his ear. The wind had picked up and the crash of the waves made it hard for them to hear each other. June put her head close to

Lily's ear and shouted, "It sounded very creepy. Something about a bed outside on a lawn that never gets wet. And I heard that it keeps happening."

"What keeps happening?" Lily asked. She had an image of beds lined up like little gravestones.

"Someone drowns in front of the bed every year," whispered June. The little smile on June's face told Lily that she was enjoying every moment of recalling the eerie story.

Clark came to a stop in front of a twelve-foot statue of Caesar. Caesar's right hand was raised, as if he owned all of the Atlantic Ocean. "Here you are, ladies. Caesar's Palace." Clark walked around to the front of the chair. June handed him the bucket of quarters. He put it down by his feet, casually draping his jeans jacket over it. Gallantly, he helped June out of the chair, then reached under the chair and returned her bucket of quarters. She took a quarter from the top and handed it to him. "And here's a tip for you," she said.

June turned to Lily. "And this is for you. For bringing me good luck." She gave Lily a fistful of quarters. Then she waved good-bye.

Lily started to count the money. There were at least fifty quarters.

She watched Clark closely. He had smiled graciously at June and didn't make fun of her for giving him such a cheap tip and Lily such a generous one.

Lily touched Clark's arm. It was cold. She felt him flinch for just a second and she wondered why. They stood awkwardly—the distance between them just a little too close. "I liked the way you treated her."

Clark hesitated for a moment, looking around. Without saying a word, he lifted his jeans jacket, revealing a bucket that had been hidden beneath his jacket, a bucket full of shiny quarters.

"But . . . but . . . ," Lily stammered. "I saw you give her back her bucket."

"Correction," said Clark. "I gave her back *a* bucket. It just wasn't the same bucket that she gave me. Until she's back on the bus, she won't notice that beneath the top layer of quarters there's nothing but buckshot wrapped in aluminum foil. Just one of the tools of the trade."

Lily took a step backward. "You mean you stole from her?"

Clark nodded.

"Why did you show me?" asked Lily.

Clark removed his sunglasses. "I just don't want you to have any illusions about me. I don't like illusions." His voice had an edge to it. He held Lily's eyes, challenging her. The green of his irises stood out against whites as clear as a child's. Lily refused to look away or to let Clark know he was making her heart race. "I don't like thieves," she said.

Clark moved in so his face was just inches from hers.

"I think you like me," he said.

His arrogance was too much for Lily. "Are you so sure that I won't turn you in?"

"I dare you to turn me in," he said.

"You dare me?" Lily repeated.

Clark nodded. He didn't look the least afraid.

"You think I won't call your bluff?" demanded Lily. The wind blew her hair around her face, annoying her. She pushed it back with one hand, balking at giving in to Clark.

Clark put his sunglasses back on. "Do you want to go get the police?" he asked.

"Yes," said Lily. She knew as soon as she said it that she was bluffing. She didn't want to go to the police. Half of her even felt like laughing. Clark was so bold. He hadn't had to show her the bucket. He could have stolen the quarters and she would never have been the wiser.

She didn't want to give him the satisfaction of knowing that she liked him—at least not yet. "You're worse than that fortune-teller back there. She would have read the old lady's palm for her money. You just filched her money from her."

"It's both stealing."

"It is not," said Lily. "The fortune-teller would have given her something—at least a little hope."

"So what? Lies about the future?"

"It's not necessarily lies."

"So you believe in fortune-tellers?"

"They're better than thieves."

"Have you ever had your palm read?" Clark asked. He picked up her palm and turned it over, tracing her life line with his finger. Lily shivered. Clark looked out at the ocean, as if he had seen something in her palm that bothered him.

Lily took her hand away. She thought about her mother and father. She wanted to keep that side of her life private for the moment.

Clark abruptly changed the subject. "Come for a swim with me."

Lily shook her head vigorously. "No."

"Why not? It's a hot day. It will feel good."

Lily didn't want to tell him that she couldn't swim—that she was afraid of the ocean. She was desperate to change the subject. "I think I'll go back to the fortune-teller. You said I cheated her." She jiggled the quarters in her hand. "This will make up for it."

Clark knew it wouldn't be easy to get her in the ocean. He knew that she couldn't swim and that she was afraid to tell him. It made him feel tender toward her. He wondered what the fortune-teller would tell her. "I'll go with you," he said abruptly.

"I don't know," said Lily. "Maybe the fortune-teller will take one look at you and realize that you're a thief." Lily stuffed the quarters in her butt pack. They felt heavy on her waist, almost like a chain.

"You're not going to let that go, are you?" asked Clark.

Lily made a face. "Look, I'm not going to call the police, but I still think it was lousy to steal from June. She was so excited about winning and now you not only stole the money from her—but you stole that excitement too. Instead of feeling like a winner when she gets on the bus she'll realize she was robbed and she'll feel like a loser."

Clark rubbed his hand over his lips. He knew plenty about feeling like a loser. In the distance, he saw June holding up her bucket of winnings for her group to admire. He picked up the original bucket and walked over to her.

Lily watched as Clark went up to June and exchanged the buckets. When he came back she said with amazement, "You gave her back her money?"

"Yes," said Clark. "I did it for you." He smiled.

3

I DID IT FOR YOU. The words rang in Lily's head. She warned herself to hold on to her emotions. She had a tendency, especially with boys, to take one warm remark and run with it clear across the field.

Clark locked up his chair and walked beside Lily along the Boardwalk, past the saltwater taffy shops and the shops selling cheap T-shirts. The Boardwalk was more crowded than before, and several of the older tourists smiled at them. Lily wondered whether they were winners or whether they just liked the way Lily and Clark looked together, both tall and fit.

Lily told herself again to slow down. Her track record with boys was far worse than her team's soccer record. All she really knew about Clark was that he stole for the kick of it. That was enough to set off warning bells. Yet Lily knew herself well enough to admit that she was attracted to him—almost too much so.

Clark stole glances at Lily as they walked, deliberately keeping quiet, giving her a chance to be alone with her thoughts. He wanted to walk with his hand in hers, but he kept his by his side. As fast as things had gone, he didn't want to hurry.

Lily looked up at him. He gave her his boyish grin.

"What's that—impish smile number two?"

Clark's lip twitched. He wasn't used to a girl seeing through him so easily. "What do you mean?" he asked.

Lily laughed at him. "I don't know. I felt like I was getting a prepackaged smile—the one you use to make girls think you're innocent."

"I guess we're already beyond that, huh?"

"Well, for one thing—I know that you're a thief." Lily shrugged. "Well, you said you didn't like illusions. I guess you meant it. What other illusions about you do you plan on shattering?"

Clark stopped smiling. He wasn't used to being teased. Lily deliberately walked on. Clark watched her. He loved the way she walked—she stretched her legs and strode with her shoulders flung back. She looked so fearless—and alive.

They stopped in front of the fortune-teller's shop. The door to the fortune-teller's shop was closed. Green beaded curtains were drawn over the windows. Clark wasn't sure that he wanted Lily to find out about her future. He certainly knew more than enough about his own. "Are you sure you want to go in?" he asked.

"Why not?" Lily asked. She enjoyed the fact that suddenly Clark seemed nervous. She wondered whether he was a little bit afraid of the fortune-teller. Lily wasn't. When other little girls were playing Go Fish, Lily was playing with her mother's tarot cards. Her mother told her that women were especially good at understanding the power of the occult. In the book that came with her first set of tarot cards, Lily had found a poem and memorized it.

The witch woman
Sees fortunes bold
Hidden thoughts
Visions old
Shame and truth
Every woman is a witch
Every witch is wise

Lily knocked on the door. The fortune-teller opened it. "I'm busy," she said.

"I can help them," said a voice. A girl not much older than Lily came to the door. She was wearing a faded tie-dyed T-shirt dress. Her fingernails and toenails were painted purple. The girl's eyes were almond shaped, and she had a shy smile.

"I'm a reader too," she told Lily and Clark. "It's okay, Ma." The older woman returned to her client.

Clark hung back. "Would you both like your palms read?" the girl asked, directing her questions to Clark. Clark shook his head.

"Why not?" teased Lily, enjoying his discomfort.

"I don't need my palm read to know *my* future," said Clark, trying to keep his voice light. The girl stared at him. She chewed on her lip. As she led them inside the storefront, she seemed to be careful not to touch Clark.

"My name is Marie," the girl said to Lily. "Would

you like your cards and palm read? I could do them both for six dollars."

Lily shook her head. "I don't have much money." Marie glanced toward the curtained room where her mother was. Clearly her mother expected her to drive a harder bargain. "How about for five?"

"How about two?" Lily countered. "That's what it says on your sign." A plastic dog bone lay on the floor underneath the table. Lily wondered where the dog was.

The girl sighed, but finally nodded. Lily unzippered her butt pack and counted out eight quarters.

Marie shuffled a worn deck of tarot cards. "Put the money across the cards and make a wish."

Lily took a deep breath. Carefully, she placed the quarters across the cards in two piles.

Lily could sense Clark standing behind her, waiting for her wish. Suddenly she felt uncomfortable, as if even making a silent wish in front of Clark would be revealing too much. She didn't want to wish for anything that had to do with love. Instead she wished for second best. Money. Having some money of her own would give her freedom.

The girl turned over the cards quickly. "You are stuck in a cycle," she said.

Lily nodded. She couldn't possibly disagree with her.

"You have a decision to make—but you don't want to make it."

Lily looked up, startled to see that Clark was

staring at the cards intently, as if he were the ques-
tioner not she.

Marie slapped down the Wheel of Fortune. The
card showed a wheel stuck between two dead branches
meaning that good fortune came at a cost. "You want
money," said Marie. Lily snorted. That didn't take
much supernatural intuition to figure out. Somebody
needing money was a standard thing for a fortune-
teller to say. However, in Lily's case, money was a
serious issue. Her mom had taken off for the summer,
leaving Lily with her aunt Andrea, somehow assuming
that everything would work out all right.

Lily's mind drifted away from the cards. She
wished she could be a chair pusher. It would be fun to
guide tourists around the Boardwalk. A faded poster
of Atlantic City in the 1920s was Scotch-taped to the
wall. Underneath were the words *On the Boardwalk of
Atlantic City . . . everything is peaches and cream on the
Boardwalk of Atlantic City*. Lily knew Atlantic City well
enough to know that it wasn't all peaches and cream.
People came to Atlantic City for the excitement. Lily
saw herself guiding hundreds on the Boardwalk—
each of them paying her—paying her for what?

Lily wasn't really listening as Marie held out the
next card in the ancient ten card spread. "This card
will stand for your inner emotions," said Marie. "It
will show your inner hopes, hidden emotions and
secret desires. Men care for you. But something or
someone is dragging you down." Marie flipped over a
card that showed a skeleton with snakes coming out

of its mouth and right eye socket. The word *Death* was written beneath the card.

Clark gave a sharp intake of breath. Marie stared at him. "I wouldn't think the Death card would scare you," Marie said softly to Clark.

"The Death card doesn't have to mean literal death," explained Lily. "It could mean sudden or unexpected change. It could be a blessing in disguise."

Clark's green eyes looked troubled.

"It's okay," Lily reassured him.

"You know tarot," said Marie to Lily. She sounded surprised.

Lily didn't answer her. She looked back up at the poster and then down at the card. She felt inspired. Even Clark, who obviously thought of himself as so cool, was afraid of the Death card. Everybody, she knew, liked to scare themselves. Suddenly Lily saw a way to make money this summer.

Marie held the tenth card dramatically above the other cards. Lily shook her head impatiently. She was anxious for the reading to be over.

Marie placed the card facedown, saying, "This is the tenth card. It shows the future—it is the ultimate card."

"Yeah, yeah," said Lily. She had heard it all before.

Marie gave her a dirty look. She flipped over the tenth and final card, showing its face. It was the Hanged Man. The man hung not from his head, but by his feet. Butterflies surrounded him, but they had all escaped from his net.

Clark looked anxiously at Lily.

"The Hanged Man is the card of sacrifice and surrender," she said to him, taking over from Marie.

"What does it mean that you got both Death and the Hanged Man?" asked Clark. Suddenly it was as if Marie were no longer in the room with them.

"It's very unusual," admitted Lily. "It means that I or someone close to me will have hard decisions to make." She stared at the spread of the cards.

Quickly Marie reshuffled the cards. "I can give you another reading, for just a couple more dollars," she said.

"That was enough," said Lily, standing up. "Thank you." She was anxious to be on her way. Even for her, both cards—Death and the Hanged Man, were a lot to handle.

"Wait," said Marie. "Your aura needs cleansing. I could do that for you too."

"And how much would that cost?" Lily asked.

"Thirty dollars," said the girl. "But you need it."

"I don't think so," said Lily. "I can cleanse my own aura. By the way, where's your dog?"

Marie looked down at the plastic bone. She picked it up quickly. "My mother would be mad if she knew Mercedes left that here," she said.

"Your mom doesn't like your dog Mercedes?" asked Lily.

"How did you know that?"

"I can read minds too," said Lily. She parted the beaded curtains and walked outside, blinking in the bright sunlight.

Clark followed her, more intrigued than ever. Lily hadn't been afraid, neither of the Death card, nor of the Hanged Man. "Do you believe in that stuff, your aura and tarot?" he asked her.

"I enjoyed getting the Wheel of Fortune card," said Lily, not really answering him. She watched the tourists going up and down the Boardwalk. "As for the rest, well, it seems like we always have decisions to make. Do you know where the library is?" she asked abruptly.

"It's not exactly one of the places where I hang out, but I think it's on Tennessee. Why do you want the library?" Clark's voice was tense.

"The wheel of fortune is about to turn. I have to take advantage."

"You are strange," said Clark.

"Is that a compliment?" Lily asked. "Or an insult?"

"A compliment," said Clark.

"Will I see you again?" Lily asked. Clark took a step backward as if she were being too bold. Lily didn't like that. It had seemed like the connection between them was so strong. She was sick of boys who thought she was too forward.

"Never mind," she said crossly.

She took off. Clark watched her go. The library! Why of all places would she go there? Then he thought of the Death card and he thought he knew. Poor Lily, she didn't realize how little control she had over her life. He couldn't believe how abruptly she had left him, nor how much he wanted to follow her. But not to the library.

He told himself to wait. Lily would be worth the wait—a girl like her didn't come around every summer.

4

LILY COULDN'T STOP THINKING ABOUT THE DROWNED BOY'S BEDROOM, COULDN'T GET THE IMAGE OF A BED ON THE LAWN OUT OF HER HEAD. June had looked like a kid going to her first horror show when she had asked about it. If there was one bored old lady out in the morning, there would be hundreds, and they all might have an appetite for the bizarre and the weird, especially if Lily could serve it up with just a touch of horror.

She locked her bike up in front of the library. She had expected the Atlantic City library to be rundown, the way most of the city was away from the casinos. But the library looked like a casino that had wandered a few blocks away from the Boardwalk. It was a beautiful building with white squat pillars. Lily checked the hours. It was open Monday to Saturday, better hours than the library in her hometown of Toms River, New Jersey. Inside, the library looked a little like a shopping mall, with skylights and a balcony looking down on the main reading room.

"Can I help you?" asked an older woman. She seemed overdressed for the library in high heels and a blue knit suit with a white silk shirt. Her hair was pulled back in a French twist. She had age spots on her hands and was thin to the point of being fragile. Only her large chocolate brown eyes softened the severity of her looks.

Lily licked her lips. She preferred to look things up herself. She had never liked it when a teacher or librarian hovered over her while she did research. "Where are the books about the history of Atlantic City, please?" she asked.

"I was born in Atlantic City," said the woman. "I still live in the house where I grew up. I know as much about the history of Atlantic City as you'll ever find in a book. What are you looking for?"

"Oh, just some exciting tidbits," Lily said.

"Have you ever heard of the flagpole sitters?"

Somehow flagpole sitters were not exactly what Lily had in mind. She was more interested in skeletons hidden behind walls, bodies buried alive, shipwrecks, drowned boys. Flagpole sitters sounded a little tame.

"I have a signed photograph of Alvin 'Shipwreck' Kelly," said the woman. "Surely you've heard of him."

Lily shook her head.

"It was in 1930. He broke his own flagpole-sitting record. He spent forty-nine days—that's almost two months—sitting on a pole."

"Why did he finally come down?" Lily couldn't help asking.

"He missed his wife."

"He could have taken her up with him. They could have gotten his-and-her flagpoles," joked Lily.

"What?"

"Nothing." So much for the lady's sense of humor. "You must be busy." Lily tried to be tactful. "Why don't you show me where the old newspaper files are and I could start with those."

Lily found a lot of stories that appealed to her humor, but not enough horror. As late as 1850, black snakes and mosquitoes far outnumbered the people on the island that would become Atlantic City. Dr. Jonathan Pitney persuaded the railroad to build a rail line from Philadelphia. He claimed that the sea air could cure all ills, and cleverly left out all mention of the mosquitoes.

Gradually, Lily found more of what she was looking for—gangsters shot in gambling dens, horses stampeding off the piers after being bitten by mosquitoes. She kept looking for something about a drowned boy's bedroom.

It was hard to avoid stories about drownings, but she found nothing about a drowned boy's bed. It was almost as if people expected teenagers to die, kids her age who had no fear of death. Most of the teenagers who drowned got only a paragraph or two of notice.

Lily was glad that neither her mother nor her aunt knew what she was doing. They would consider it morbid. She also knew if she looked hard enough she'd find the obituary for her father.

She came across one drowning that actually made the front page. GURNEY BOY PRESUMED DROWNED.

The photo was blurry and showed the boy with his mother. The mother was all high cheekbones and as thin as a model. The boy's eyes looked huge in his face. His mouth was drawn down in a frown. He was dressed in a suit and narrow tie, and although the photo was too vague to make out his features, his body posture made it clear he was uncomfortable.

Lily read his obituary. It told her more about his mother's charitable contributions to the town than it did about the boy, nothing other than the fact that he was a senior at some boarding school, who always returned to Atlantic City for the summer.

Lily wondered if there was some secret about him that the newspaper was hiding. Maybe he had been drunk or did drugs. The light changed in the skylight above her as a cloud blocked the sun. She started to rewind the microfilm. She was getting tired, and the library would be closing soon.

Then a small paragraph caught her eye. It was dated just a few weeks after the obituary for Mrs. Gurney's son.

NEIGHBORS OBJECT TO DROWNED BOY'S BEDROOM

As much as Katherine Gurney's neighbors respect her grief at the death of her son, they are concerned that the bed that she has placed on the lawn is a nuisance attraction.

"Of course, any parent would sympathize with her tragedy, but she seems to believe that her son will return to the bedroom if it is outside," said Mr. Cannon.

"You know how people are," said his wife, Mrs. Joyce Cannon. "My son tells me that kids are already telling ghost stories about the bedroom—some silly story about how the bed stays dry even when it rains."

"It's the kind of thing that can drive down property values," added Mr. Cannon.

Bingo! Lily thought to herself. She rubbed her hand over her face. The drowned boy's bedroom.

She kept going, reading obituaries, almost daring herself to find her father's. She didn't get that far. The year after the Gurney boy's bed had been placed on his lawn, she came across the neighbors named Cannon again, but this time the tragedy was theirs.

JIMMY CANNON'S BODY WASHED ASHORE

Jimmy Cannon, age sixteen, drowned. His body washed ashore just yards from his front lawn. His grief-stricken parents were on the beach. A riptide grabbed him. They tried to rescue him, but by the time his father reached the body, his son was already dead. Father and mother tried to resuscitate their child but to no avail.

Katherine Gurney, their next-door neighbor, was particularly distraught. She too was swimming in front of her house at the time and couldn't reach him to save him. "He was a lovely boy. Ever since my son's death, he had been a comfort to me, coming over for lemonade, keeping me company." Mrs. Gurney, who just spearheaded the drive for the new hospital wing, lost her own son tragically in the same manner almost exactly a year ago.

* * *

Lily knew all about riptides and undertows. She glanced up at the skylight. The cloud had turned an ugly dark gray. She wrote down the addresses of the Gurney and Cannon homes and returned the microfilm.

She didn't want to read about her father's drowning in the paper. Her mother had kept the articles anyhow—tucked into the book that people had signed at his funeral. Lily never opened that book.

The library had computers for people to use. Quickly Lily sat and typed in her copy for a flyer. Tales of Terror on the Boardwalk . . . Lily laughed out loud at what she was typing. Finished, she sent the copy to the printer. She was concentrating so hard that she didn't even realize that the librarian was standing over her.

Lily rolled her chair back from the computer, hoping that the woman wouldn't read what was on the screen.

"What are you working on?" asked the lady.

"It's just a little project I'm doing."

Before Lily could stop her, the woman went to the printer to see what was coming out. "You don't mind, do you, dear?" she asked as she brought Lily the printed copy.

She glanced down at the big type that the computer called "ghost writing." It made the letters with shadows and squiggly lines. "'Shiver and lose weight at the same time—a trip so far off the beaten path—

you might never come back. Led by Lily Potter.' So that's your name. Well, you'll need more than one copy, won't you?"

"The library charges ten cents a copy. I was hoping to find a place on Atlantic Avenue that would do it cheaper."

The woman smiled at her. "Is money important to you?" she asked.

It means freedom, Lily thought to herself. Out loud she said, "I need the money for college," knowing it sounded more acceptable. She spaced her words evenly. Only people who had never worried about money would ask something so stupid as, "Is money important to you?"

"Go on, dear, print out a hundred copies on the library's machine. I'll take care of it."

Lily swallowed her pride. A hundred copies would save her money that she didn't have. "Thank you," she said.

The woman smiled. "It's my pleasure," she said. "I'll reimburse the library. So that's why you're so interested in Atlantic City history? You like horror stories?"

Lily shrugged.

"Shrugging is unbecoming," said the woman. She patted Lily's shoulders as if willing them to stay down. Lily rolled her eyes, wondering whether getting free copies was worth having this woman correct her posture.

"And don't roll your eyes. They can freeze that

way," she said.

Lily laughed. "I don't think that's true."

The woman looked serious. "If you want to be a success in this world, it's important to break bad habits, like shrugging and rolling your eyes. Discipline in appearance is very important." She gave Lily a tight little smile.

Just another adult with rules for teenagers, thought Lily. It never ceased to amaze her how adults felt free to tell teenagers how to behave. If Lily suggested that the woman had too much hair spray on her hair, or that the color lipstick she was wearing didn't go with the blush on her cheeks, she'd think Lily incredibly rude. But she thought nothing of giving free advice that Lily had not asked for.

Lily gave her a tight smile back.

"You're a pretty girl when you smile," said the librarian.

There she goes again, thought Lily. The same adults who tell you to smile are never the ones who really want you to have a good time. They want you smiling, but they don't want you laughing. Lily knew what she wanted. She wanted her flyers and she wanted out of there. She kept smiling until the copier spat out one hundred copies of her flyer.

The woman stood over her, helping her stack them into a neat pile. Lily struggled not to let her impatience show. She figured the old lady was lonely. Lily's mother would have found something nice and compassionate to say to her. But she made

Lily nervous, made her feel self-conscious. Lily couldn't wait to get out of the library. She stuffed the flyers in her butt pack and thanked the woman.

"Good luck on your tour," said the woman. She smiled. Her lipstick was beginning to feather, emphasizing the age lines in her lips. Lily felt that she should do something to show her appreciation. She took out one of her flyers and gave it to the old woman. "Maybe you'll want to join me," she said. "You won't have to pay."

The woman smiled. "I don't think it's exactly my cup of tea, but thank you."

Lily left the library and deposited her flyers at the hotels of the casinos. She was exhausted by the time she finished. She headed toward her aunt's apartment.

5

THE SKY HAD A GREENISH CAST TO IT, LIKE THE BOTTOM OF A DIRTY SWIMMING POOL. The ocean wasn't even pretending that it was a benign and welcoming presence. Bolts of lightning as thick as a man's arm shot into the sea, just a mile offshore.

Clark stood under the statue of Julius Caesar, getting little protection from the rain. The tourists around Clark yelped and scurried back into the casinos, passing him as if he too were made of stone, an inanimate object not to be bothered with. A lightning bolt lit up the Boardwalk as the rain slanted in from the ocean, stinging Clark's eyes. His T-shirt stuck to his body and his wet jeans hugged his legs. He left Caesar's shelter and walked down the Boardwalk, past all the casinos. Underneath the boardwalk, Clark could have found relief from the rain. It was where he kept his bedroll, hidden out of sight, his temporary home. But right now, he wasn't interested in shelter. He just kept walking until he reached some of the houses that still existed along the Boardwalk. These houses seemed so private, yet anyone walking along the Boardwalk could see into them.

He thought about Lily. She had asked to see him again, and he had flubbed it—just like a typical teenage twit. He was neither, certainly not a typical teenager and definitely not a twit.

Every summer Clark chose someone, and none lasted longer than the summer. He had picked Lily out on the Boardwalk, expecting her to be just that, this summer's choice. He was tempted to let her get away. That was why he had backed off when she asked if she could see him again. Yet, he knew himself. He liked her too much to let her go. He'd find her again. He'd have to search the Boardwalk, but that was one of the glories of Atlantic City. Sooner or later you always ran into the person you wanted to see on the Boardwalk. He would just have to find a way to make it sooner. A burst of thunder roared, startling even him.

The same clap of thunder made Lily jump. She dashed for her aunt's apartment, hoping to beat the storm, but she miscalculated. By the time she got there, she was soaked.

Aunt Andrea was waiting for her, her hair braided and wrapped in a crown around her head. Pearls and rhinestones were woven into the braids. "Honey," she said. "I was beginning to worry about you out in the rain."

"I was at the library," said Lily.

Aunt Andrea handed Lily a towel and gently massaged Lily's hair, drying it. "The library? Only you would come to Atlantic City and go to the library. I thought you would spend the day on the Boardwalk."

"I did," said Lily. "But then I got an idea to make money."

"Oh, sweetie, I told you jobs are impossible to get

in Atlantic City. I'm lucky to be a waitress." She put down the towel. She patted her own hair. "I got this do just so it will attract tips."

"And it's quite spectacular," added Lily. She loved Aunt Andrea's changes of hairstyle. It was a sign of her aunt's optimism—get a new haircut, get a new life. No matter how down on her luck Aunt Andrea might be, she never seemed downhearted. Of all the people in Lily's family, Aunt Andrea always had time for her. When Andrea found out that Lily's mother wanted to go away for the summer, Aunt Andrea had made it sound as if Lily would be doing *her* a favor by keeping her company.

Lily watched a lightning bolt hit the water on the inlet. The bright white light was so sharp it gave the apartment a strobelike effect. For a second, Lily was disoriented. The portrait of her father shimmered above the couch. It was a photograph tinted with oil paints and it gave his skin color a strange coppery look. Lily's father was about her age in the portrait, maybe a year older, eighteen at the oldest. He was on the beach, his arm around his little sister Andrea, half protecting her. He had a huge grin on his face.

Aunt Andrea followed her gaze. "I wish that he had lived to see you now," she said. "He'd think you were so beautiful."

Lily said nothing.

"Your dad would be so happy that you're finally spending a summer at his beach. He loved the water so much."

"What's for dinner?" Lily asked. She didn't want to talk about her father. She turned away from the portrait.

"I thought we'd go out tonight. Celebrate your being here. I don't have to be at work tonight until eight o'clock. I'll take you where they've got the best spaghetti and meatballs in town."

The storm had passed by the time Lily took a shower and changed into a pair of black jeans and a white shirt. "Is this restaurant too fancy for jeans?" she asked.

Aunt Andrea shook her head. "Do you think I want fancy before spending hours on my feet serving people in the casino? It's not fancy, but you'll love it."

Aunt Andrea took Lily's arm as they walked by the ocean. The casinos threw long shadows on the Boardwalk. With the storm abated, people had come out for strolls, hoping for better luck at the next casino.

"They're all here for vacation," said Lily. "But they don't look very happy."

"Well, gambling is only fun when you win—and most of these people are not going to win," said Aunt Andrea. "But hope is eternal, and hope keeps them going. It keeps me going too. I've signed up to become a dealer. I'm way down on the waiting list, though. You have to go to a school to learn, but if I make it, I'd have a chance to make some good money for a change."

"That's great," said Lily, not really listening. She watched a teenage boy and girl carrying a duffel bag between them. The boy and girl were laughing. The boy dropped the duffel and took the girl in his arms. Their bodies rubbed against each other. It was as if they couldn't stand being separated, not even by a duffel bag.

Aunt Andrea followed Lily's gaze. "You're not still brooding about that boy back home, are you? The one you broke up with?"

"Mom told you about Reggie?"

"She just said not to mind if you were moody the first few days."

"Reggie broke up with me. He said that we were getting too involved."

Aunt Andrea laughed. "I'm sorry," she said. "I just can't believe that guys are still using that line. You'd think they'd invent something new."

"I wish there was a law that said boyfriends are not allowed to break up with you at the beginning of a summer, just the end," Lily said. "Or, I guess if I'm honest, I just wish I had done it first. I hate feeling like a doormat."

"Sweetie, any guy that makes you feel like a doormat isn't worth it."

Lily laughed. "I'll remember that. At least you make more sense than Mom. You know what she said when she heard Reggie broke up with me? 'Lily, you must learn to hold with an open hand.'"

"Well, your mom has a different way of looking at the world," said Aunt Andrea. Lily knew she was trying to be diplomatic.

"Yeah, I'll say," said Lily. "I hope she's enjoying her 'vision quest' in New Mexico. Before she left, she told me to think of Reggie as a learning experience. I must learn that if I 'clutch tight, love slips through my fingers, struggles free, or dies.' Thank you for that fortune cookie, Mom. You know what I think. If you love someone, set them free—if they don't come back, hunt them down and shoot them."

Aunt Andrea laughed. "Where did you get that?"

"I saw it on a T-shirt on the Boardwalk."

"Don't be bitter. There's something to say for your mom's words. Listen, I know what it's like to be dumped by someone you've clung to."

"Great. I'm following in the family tradition." Lily immediately regretted her words. Andrea had been divorced twice. Her first husband had run out on her when they were only twenty. Her second husband had left her just six months ago. That was when she had moved to Atlantic City from Philadelphia.

"Bad luck in love is not a family tradition. Your mom and dad had a wonderful marriage. They laughed all the time. Your dad loved to laugh."

"Was he as spacey as Mom sometimes is?"

"Not exactly, though I don't like you calling your mom spacey. She's always managed to take care of you."

"I didn't mean to put her down," Lily said quickly. "I know Mom isn't always the dingbat people think she is." Lily looked out at the sea. She didn't want to talk about her mother anymore. One of the reasons she loved being with Aunt Andrea was that she wasn't her parent. Aunt Andrea's advice was always easier to take than advice from her mother. She smiled at her aunt. "I like being in Atlantic City with you," she said.

Her aunt put her arm through Lily's. "Me too," she said. "I always feel as if I'm walking through a Monopoly game as I walk the streets."

Lily looked at the private homes along the Boardwalk. "It's funny," she said. "I just don't think of real houses belonging in Atlantic City. Just the little ones from the Monopoly board."

"That's what I thought when I first moved here. Most of the tourists never come to this area." Aunt Andrea stopped and rested her elbows on the railing and looked out at the ocean. "Your dad loved the sea more than anybody I've ever known. He was always picking up driftwood from the high-tide line. They were just sticks to me, but your dad would make up stories about where those sticks had been. He was always a dreamer—I think that's what made him fall in love with your mother. They were more alike than people realized."

"That's what Mom says," Lily agreed. Her father had died not far from here, when they had all gone to the shore, just a little north of where Lily was now standing. Lily's mother had been helping her make a castle by letting the wet sand slip through her fingers to make turrets and walls from drips of sand. They had their backs to the ocean. They never saw the undertow that grabbed Lily's father and pulled him under. If he shouted, they didn't hear it.

Lily could still remember waiting on the beach as the sun set, her mother pacing back and forth, somehow convinced that Lily's father had just gone for a long swim. His body washed up over five miles away.

Lily turned away from the ocean. From underneath the boards, Clark recognized Lily's voice as she walked with her aunt after the storm. It had been fun to follow them, eavesdropping. Although he rarely believed in luck, he took it as a good omen that he was able to find her so quickly. He had liked hearing that Lily had been recently dumped by a guy. It made her more vulnerable.

He guessed that there was a tragic story behind Lily's reluctance to talk about her father and her fear of the ocean. Knowing her weaknesses could come in handy, and Lily definitely had some weaknesses worth probing.

When they had turned off the Boardwalk to go to the restaurant, Clark climbed up and nimbly jumped the railing. He walked until he came to the drowned boy's bedroom. He stared at the bed on the lawn. The bed was very familiar to him. He knew it well.

When Lily had asked him about it, he had pretended not to hear her. He hadn't wanted to tell her about it too soon. The drowned boy's bed stood on the lawn, as if it were just waiting for someone to sleep on it. The boy's mother claimed that it sat there as a symbol of her grief. But Clark didn't trust either symbols or mothers. Mothers could be liars and thieves. Being a mother didn't give you immunity, especially mothers who refused to let go.

6

THE ISLAND THAT ATLANTIC CITY SITS ON IS SHAPED LIKE A PORK CHOP. Lily and her aunt were down in the bone area, away from the big casinos. Here, just a few blocks away from the wealthy homes on the ocean, were the restaurants and shops that only residents knew about and few tourists ever ventured. Aunt Andrea led Lily into Angelo's, an old wooden restaurant with white trim around the door. "This is it," she said. Inside, the dark wooden walls exuded the smell of tomato sauce. "Sonny goes out and picks his own tomatoes every day," Aunt Andrea explained.

"Sonny? I thought this place was called Angelo's."

"Sonny inherited it from Angelo," said Aunt Andrea, waving to a couple of people she knew. They sat in a booth. "Sonny, this is my niece," she said to the man who stood ready to take their order. He was a large man with friendly bushy eyebrows.

Sonny stretched out his hand. Lily shook it. "Your aunt is a great addition to this town. And I should know. I've lived here all my life."

Lily liked Sonny, and she wondered how friendly Aunt Andrea had gotten with him. "Tonight, you should have the lasagna," said Sonny. "I made it fresh this morning. Green noodles—ricotta—tomatoes—it's the best."

"We'll have it," said Aunt Andrea.

Within minutes he brought over two steaming plates of lasagna. "Thanks," said Lily. She thought about her tour. She wanted to start it right away, but she needed more details if she wasn't going to just wing it. "Excuse me," Lily asked Sonny. "Have you ever heard of a house with the drowned boy's bed on the lawn?" she asked.

"Mrs. Gurney's place," said Sonny.

"Is that the same Mrs. Gurney who gives to all the charities?" asked Aunt Andrea. "She owns a piece of the casino where I work."

"The same," said Sonny.

"I've seen pictures of her," said Aunt Andrea. "She's gorgeous."

"Yeah, she was some piece of work in her younger days. I used to bartend her parties. Let me tell you, that classy-looking broad could put them away. She definitely liked to have a good time."

"In the photos I've seen she didn't look like a drinker," said Aunt Andrea.

"No, she could hide it. People look at her and see what they want to see—the grand lady who gives money away like it was going out of style. Yet, believe me, she had her wild side. Why shouldn't she give some of her money away? She has a fortune. She owned most of the land under two thirds of the casinos."

"She is one beautiful woman," said Andrea.

"You must have seen old photos," said Sonny. "She

refuses to have her picture taken since her son died."

Lily ate her lasagna. It tasted delicious, but she wasn't interested in Mrs. Gurney's drinking or her charities. "Can you tell me more about the bed?" she interrupted.

"It's not far from here. Let me tell you, a lot of people thought it was ghoulish for her to put that bed outside. They tried to get her to bring it inside. But with money like that, I guess she can do anything she wants."

"What does she do when it rains?" asked Andrea. "Hire servants to change the sheets?"

"I guess you heard that old legend that it never rains on the bed," said Sonny.

"Is it true?" Lily asked.

Sonny hesitated. "Well, I've walked by and it looks dry—but I always figured Mrs. Gurney had the money to do something special to it, you know. What I really wish she would do something about cordoning that area off. It's such a wicked undertow in front of her house. That entire area of the beach is a death-trap. I don't think we've ever gotten through a summer without some kid drowning in that area. . . ."

Suddenly, Lily's stomach felt queasy.

"You look a little pale," said Aunt Andrea.

Lily put down her fork. Sonny looked anxious. "Is something wrong with my lasagna?" he asked.

Lily shook her head. "It's delicious. The portions are huge."

"A big healthy girl like you needs to eat."

Lily was rarely sick to her stomach. Her friends all told her she had the appetite of a horse. She took a second bite. Sonny watched until she took a third and fourth bite. Then he left them. The cheese tasted gooey. She pictured a bed lying on the lawn. Her stomach heaved. Then it was as if the bed were in the restaurant. The booth next to her had sheets on it, neatly tucked in with hospital corners.

She blinked. She must be hallucinating. She pushed the lasagna aside. She couldn't eat. She almost never got sick to her stomach. She shivered involuntarily. Her mother used to tell her that when that happened, "Somebody walked over her grave."

Lily looked at the booth next to them. It was just a booth again, not a bed. She felt cold and damp, even though it was a hot summer night.

Aunt Andrea looked at her with concern. "You're shivering," she said.

"It's nothing," Lily said. "I'm all right." Her teeth were chattering as if she had been swimming in the ocean.

"You're not all right," said Aunt Andrea.

Lily swallowed. She didn't want her aunt to be worried. She forced herself to relax, and the surprising thing about it was that it worked. The shivers stopped.

When they finished, Aunt Andrea paid the check. She patted her elaborate hairdo. "I'd better be getting to the casino," she said, looking at her watch. "I don't have time to walk. I'll take the bus. It goes right back to our house. Do you want to take it with me?"

Lily took a deep breath. The air felt fresh after the storm. The sky was a beautiful dusky blue. She didn't feel like sitting in Aunt Andrea's apartment all night, watching television. She also needed to check out the sights for her tour, particularly the drowned boy's bedroom. "I'll walk back along the Boardwalk. Okay?"

"All right," said Aunt Andrea. "But don't walk the Boardwalk after dark by yourself. It's dangerous." Aunt Andrea gave her a hug and kiss. Lily hugged her back, careful not to mess her hair. "Thanks for dinner and the talk," Lily said. "No more doormat for me."

"You're nobody's idea of a doormat," said Aunt Andrea.

7

LILY WAS NERVOUS. She hadn't wanted to tell her aunt about her brief hallucination in the restaurant, but the image of the bed haunted her. She couldn't wait to see it herself. She walked the few short blocks back up to the Boardwalk quickly. She could see the neon signs of the casinos in the distance. She turned away from them, reaching into her butt pack, and pulling out her small notebook.

She checked the numbers on the house in front of her and realized she was standing in front of Jimmy Cannon's home. The house was built like a modern French chateau. Two cement Doberman pinschers guarded the pool in front of the house. Stretching out from the pool area was a perfectly mowed lawn with dice-shaped bushes on the side. The name Jimmy had sounded so simple. She had envisioned a little beach cottage, not this mansion.

She held her breath. She knew that the drowned boy's bedroom was right next door. She forced herself to go look.

The bed was shaded by a red maple tree. It sat just a few feet from the Boardwalk. The headboard was made out of reddish wood and so was the footboard. A red Indian blanket lay neatly folded at the foot of the bed. Fresh sheets had been tucked in with neat hospital corners. It was so much smaller and sadder than Lily had expected. It looked even more bizarre than she imagined, just sitting on the middle of the lawn.

The house itself looked lived in. The shades were up, and most of the rooms had white curtains that fluttered in the breeze. A few of the windows had stained glass. The borders of Mrs. Gurney's lawn were planted with wild roses.

Lily couldn't look at the bed anymore. Almost against her will, she turned and gazed out at the ocean. The ocean was calm now. She saw a little girl about seven or eight playing in the shallow waves. Someone was swimming just a little beyond the breakers. She watched a moment. She didn't think the little girl should be by herself. She was relieved when the girl walked out of the water and started to dig a hole in the sand. Lily took a deep breath. The girl was definitely safer out of the water.

What am I? The baby-sitter of the western world? Lily thought to herself. The little girl really wasn't her problem. She turned away from the beach and made herself look again at the bed on the lawn in front of the Gurney mansion, trying to memorize details to point out on her tour. It was nearly dark now and concealed floodlights threw shadows of the red maple onto the red brick. The shadows of leaves moved in the warm summer breeze. How strange that Mrs. Gurney would light the bed at night—as if it truly were a beacon for her son to come home to.

Suddenly someone shouted from the beach. The little girl was jumping up and down and pointing out at the ocean. Lily squinted. She could just make out the lone swimmer. He or she, Lily couldn't tell whether it was a man or a woman, was thrashing about, obviously trying to swim in, but making no headway.

"Jimmy went too far out! Jimmy went too far out!" screamed the girl.

Lily jumped over the railing and fell into the sand, about four feet down. Her legs absorbed her weight and she sprinted toward the little girl. The sand was hard from the rain and it made it easier to run on. She was panting when she got to the edge of the ocean.

"Where's the lifeguard?" she demanded of the little girl.

"I don't know," wailed the little girl. "Jimmy's my older brother. Jimmy asked somebody and they said it was fine to swim here. He went too far out. Go get him."

Lily watched the bobbing head. "I can't swim!" Lily admitted. The little girl started to wail. Lily stepped gingerly into the ocean. "Go!" screamed the little girl.

"HELP!" Lily yelled at the top of her lungs. She looked around, but this area of the beach was deserted. She started to wade into the waves. The water lapped at her waist. She cursed herself for never learning how to swim. She knew it was stupid to try to rescue the boy herself. If she drowned, she would do the swimmer no good, and her mother would never recover from another death. Yet Lily had to do something. She felt the undertow drag at her legs, lifting them up. She had a moment of panic, but she kept her eye on the swimmer, determined somehow to not let him disappear.

Suddenly she heard splashing to her left. She saw someone dive into the water. With crisp clean strokes, the rescuer broke free of the breakers.

He swam parallel to the beach, keeping his eye on the swimmer in trouble. When he was just at the right angle, he thrust himself forward and grabbed the thrashing swimmer and pulled him out of the grasp of the undertow.

"Jimmy! Jimmy! He's got Jimmy!" shouted the little girl.

"Stay on shore!" commanded Lily. She waded farther out to try to help the rescuer. The water lapped at Lily's chest, pulling her up on her tiptoes.

The rescuer pushed Jimmy toward her. Jimmy had swallowed salt water and he was gasping and heaving. His chin butted up and hit Lily's. Her neck jerked back. For a second she almost blacked out. She staggered, but she didn't lose her balance. She put her arm around the boy's waist. The rescuer stood up and took Jimmy's other side.

"Clark!" shouted Lily, suddenly realizing that she wasn't at all surprised that it was he.

Clark didn't answer. He was breathing hard.

Lily helped them both onto the beach. Jimmy fell

onto the sand, on all fours. He heaved up the salt water he had swallowed.

"Oh, gross!" said the little girl.

"Is he all right?" Lily asked Clark.

Clark flopped down on his back to catch his breath.

Lily bent over the boy called Jimmy. She patted his back. He rolled over and wiped his mouth. He was about thirteen with freckles. His ears stuck out and his nose was too big for his face. "Thanks," he mumbled.

Clark lay still on the sand. His chest was heaving up and down. "Are *you* all right?" Lily asked. Clark still didn't answer.

"Man, I thought I was gone for sure," said Jimmy. "I swam as hard as I could, but I just kept going farther out." Jimmy coughed again and phlegm ran down his chin. Lily patted her pockets, and came up with a soaking wet tissue. It shredded in her hand.

"Here," said Clark. He gave Jimmy a white handkerchief that he had in his jeans' pocket. Clark kept it in a plastic bag and it was dry. Lily stared at the handkerchief. Clark was such an extraordinary mixture. One moment he was working scams on tourists, the next he was rescuing them, even offering a dry handkerchief from his pocket. If not for Clark, Jimmy would be dead. And what about her? She shuddered as she remembered the feel of the water up to her chest, forcing her off her toes.

"What were you doing swimming here?" Clark asked.

"I was trying to rescue the boy," Lily answered.

"That nice lady said it was okay to swim here," chirped Jimmy's little sister.

"You told him that!" Clark snapped at Lily.

"Not her," said the little girl. "The lady who told us was *much* older. Look, there she is."

Both Clark and Lily followed the girl's pudgy finger. Up on the Boardwalk, a woman was leaning against the railing, looking out. She was wearing a large straw sunbonnet that hid her face. When she saw Clark and Lily staring at her, she quickly turned and walked away.

"Excuse me," said Clark. Suddenly he was sprinting up the beach, running fast on the hard sand. He ran at an angle to the woman. He took the stairs up to the Boardwalk two at a time. He grabbed the woman's arm. Lily saw Clark spin the woman around angrily. The two stood arguing, their faces close to each other.

Then Clark abruptly vaulted back over the railing. Lily shaded her hand in front of her face, trying to see through the rays of the setting sun in the west. The woman was staring back at her.

The little girl tugged at Lily's T-shirt. "Jimmy's throwing up again."

"We'd better get him where he can warm up," said Lily. "Where are you staying?"

"I'm okay," said Jimmy. "Come on, Kristen. We're staying at Caesar's Palace."

Without even thanking Lily, or waiting for Clark to return to thank *him* for saving his life, Jimmy walked down the beach. Suddenly Lily was very angry. "You know, you should be more careful," she shouted. "A boy named Jimmy drowned here already. And I hear that every year someone drowns around here. You shouldn't have been swimming alone."

Jimmy turned. "I told you—the lady said it was okay."

Lily turned and looked back up at the Boardwalk where the woman was still staring at her. What kind of a woman told a kid to swim in a dangerous undertow?

8

"WHO WAS THAT WOMAN?" Lily asked when Clark returned.

Clark didn't answer. He wanted to take Lily in his arms, and feel her warmth. He looked at her. She had plunged into the ocean to try to rescue a stranger, even though he knew she must have been terrified.

Lily stared at Clark's face. He looked almost as if he had seen a ghost, or worse, was a ghost. "Clark, are you all right? What did you say to that woman? Why did she tell Jimmy to swim here? Sonny, the guy at the restaurant, said this area has a horrible undertow."

"Why did you go in the water?" Clark asked Lily, ignoring her questions.

"I couldn't let him drown. Why won't you tell me who that woman was?"

Clark closed his eyes. "Lily, please . . . ," begged Clark. Lily knew he wasn't going to tell her more. "You saved that boy's life," she said, touching Clark's shoulder.

Clark looked down at her. He shook his head sadly. Clark realized that in the adrenaline high of the rescue, it would be almost effortless to take her now—to lead her back in the ocean. He shivered.

Lily looked at him. "You've got goosebumps all over."

"I'm all right," he said. His teeth started chattering.
Lily took the jeans jacket that Clark had thrown off as
he dived in the ocean and put it around his shoulders.
"Come on," she said. She led him up the stairs to the
Boardwalk, right in front of the Gurney mansion.

Lily stood staring at the bed, mesmerized. In the
moonlight, the sheets from the bed on the lawn shimmered. Her feet felt bolted to the Boardwalk. "Have
you ever touched it?" she asked unexpectedly. Before
Clark could answer, as if by their own accord, her feet
moved toward the bed. "I want to get closer."

"No!" The word burst out of Clark.

Lily stared at him. "What's wrong?"

"I don't want you near that bed," he said through
gritted teeth.

"Why?"

"Just . . . trust me."

Lily didn't answer him. She seemed bewitched by
the bed. "Do you really think it never rains on it?"

"Leave it alone," Clark warned.

Lily climbed on top of the railing, separating the
lawn from the public Boardwalk. Her eyes gleamed in
the floodlights from the dead boy's bed. She jumped
onto the lawn, falling forward. "Come on," she whispered. She tiptoed across the lawn, closer to the
floodlights. She took the edge of her T-shirt and
unscrewed the floodlight.

"For god's sake, Lily. What are you doing? Please,
let's get out of here." But he joined her on the lawn,
next to the bed.

Someone had tucked the sheets and blankets in

tight. Lily reached out a hand to touch the bed. Clark grabbed her hand. "Lily, don't." She laughed at him. Her laugh was the last thing that he had expected.

She sat gingerly on the bed. The springs squeaked. She was afraid of the bed, but the fear excited her.

She tucked her hands between her legs. She left one hand tucked under her thigh and touched the top sheet. Clark watched her, spellbound. She looked up at him. "Come sit on it," she whispered.

Clark closed his eyes for a second. A groan came out of him.

Lily looked up at him. "What's wrong?" she asked.

He had tears in the corner of his eyes. He started to sweat despite his chill from being in the ocean.

"Lily . . ." He took a step forward. Lily took his hand, but he wouldn't sit on the bed. He tried to pull her up to him. Lily leaned back. The bedsprings creaked. She tried to pull Clark onto the bed with her, but he resisted.

Clark jumped away from her. "No, Lily, don't."

Lily looked down at the bed, as if suddenly remembering where she was. She was on the drowned boy's bed.

"Lily," urged Clark. "Get off that bed. Now!" Clark's voice was commanding.

9

AS SHE GOT UP FROM THE BED, LILY FELT A PANG OF DIS-
APPOINTMENT, ALMOST REJECTION. She and Clark
walked wordlessly down the Boardwalk. Lily couldn't
speak. She felt angry with Clark, and yet she didn't
know why.

When they reached her aunt's apartment, Clark
followed her up the stairs. It was a lot more dilapi-
dated than he had expected. The stairs creaked under
his footsteps, and the door to the apartment was
flimsy. He realized that any burglar could knock it
down with one good kick.

Lily went to put on dry clothes. When she
returned she noticed that Clark's eyes looked
exhausted. There were dark brown shadows under his
eyebrows. Her anger softened toward him. "How
about a cup of tea?" Lily asked him.

"A cup of tea sounds good." Clark was aware of
Lily's anger, but he had chosen to ride it out, like a
storm at sea.

She went to the kitchen and put on the hot water.
"Would you rather have some soup?" she asked. She
got clam chowder out of the refrigerator and put it in
a saucepan. "My aunt makes great clam chowder." She
came back into the living room holding a mug with

chamomile tea in it. Clark was staring at the portrait of Lily's father with Andrea.

"Who's that?" he asked. "He's handsome."

"My dad."

"Is he from around here?"

"Close. Wildwood. My parents met on the Boardwalk. Mom got a splinter. Dad helped her get the splinter out of her toe. Mom claims there is such a thing as love at first sight—or at least love at first splinter."

Clark looked at Lily above the steam from his mug. He could see the resemblance to her father. Clark glanced at the portrait again. The man in the portrait was vibrant—at ease with himself and happy. Lily should be like that, not the zombie she was on the bed.

Lily felt uncomfortable as Clark studied the portrait of her father. She dreaded the fuss that some people made when they learned how her father died. It always seemed like the wrong people wanted to know about it.

"My father's dead," said Lily tersely. She watched for Clark's reaction.

Clark met her eyes over his steaming cup of tea. "What happened?" he asked, although he already knew. He tried to keep his face still so that Lily would open up to him.

Lily met his gaze. She couldn't remember Reggie wanting to know. "He drowned. I was making a sand castle on the beach." Suddenly Lily shivered. She remembered her feeling of panic when she had plunged into the ocean to rescue Jimmy. "I'd better check on the soup."

Clark followed her into the kitchen. He stood very close to her. There really wasn't enough room for two people to turn around in the kitchen.

He took the bowl of soup from her. Their hands touched. "So what's your mother like?" he asked.

"My mother believes in stuff that some people make fun of," said Lily. "But how come you get to ask me all these questions, and I don't get to ask you any?"

Clark smiled. "Ask away." He sat at the table with his bowl of soup. "Aren't you hungry?" he asked.

Lily shook her head. "I ate a huge dinner. Where do you live? Where is your family from?"

Clark looked down at his soup. "There's just my mom. I don't live with her. I ran away years ago."

"Years ago?" repeated Lily. "You must have been just a little kid. Where did you go?"

Clark's head jerked up. "To the beach," he said.

"You've been living on the beach by yourself all these years?"

Clark shrugged. "Maybe I'm lying. Maybe I'm an alien sent to spy on you earthlings and to pick out one of you to bring back to my planet as my bride."

"Very funny, alien," said Lily, laughing. Clark looked up. Lily's feistiness and humor were back. She had seemed so strange and haunted on the drowned boy's bed. He liked her better human.

She poured herself a cup of tea. Clark grinned at her. "You always act like you're laughing at a private joke that you won't share," Lily said to him. Clark held his spoon in midair. Lily had come closer to the truth than he expected. She met his gaze without looking away.

"You're no doormat," he said softly to himself.

"What did you say?" Lily asked, shocked by his choice of words.

"Nothing." He knew he had to change the subject quickly. He didn't want to have to admit to Lily that he eavesdropped on her from under the Boardwalk. He pretended to shiver.

"You're still chilled," said Lily, distracted as Clark had hoped. She brought him a quilt from her bed and wrapped it around him. He took her hand. She put her hand up to touch him on the cheek. Her fingers felt soft and warm. "Why won't you tell me what you were shouting at that woman?"

"Does your mother drink?" Clark asked unexpectedly.

"Is that what's wrong with your mother?" Lily asked. "Is that why you left when you were so young?"

Clark didn't answer, but Lily knew the answer must be yes.

"My mother's a sick woman," Clark said finally. "When I was little, I couldn't figure out what was going on in our house. Mama got headaches. Mama had to sleep a lot. I thought maybe she was dying. I used to think that she was so sick that she *needed* to have breakfast in bed. It's so weird when you're a kid. You keep thinking you understand, but you don't, and the rules keep changing. She had one set of rules for when she was sober and another for when she was drunk."

"I'm sorry," said Lily. "What about your dad?"

"Mom divorced him when I was two. He lives somewhere in South America."

"Don't you see him?"

"I've never even met him," said Clark. "Mom wanted a child without the hassle of a man thinking that he should have a say in the upbringing," said Clark. Lily had the feeling he was unconsciously mimicking his mother's voice.

"It sounds tough," said Lily. "So that's why you ran away."

"Basically I don't think anybody would live with my mom if there was a choice. As soon as I could choose—I split. I made the Boardwalk my home." Clark raised his eyebrows. "Sorry you asked?"

"About what?"

"My life history," said Clark.

"No," said Lily. "I'm not."

"I'm not sorry you asked either." He stood up and shrugged off the quilt. "I should get going." Then he saw one of her flyers. "What's this?" he asked.

"I'm going to give tours on the Boardwalk."

"'Secret tales of terror,'" read Clark. "'The ghosts

and ghouls of Atlantic City.' This is what you're going to show people?"

Lily nodded. She felt a little bit embarrassed. "Why not? I got the idea while we were together at the fortune-teller's. I did the research in the library. I found articles about the drowned boy's bedroom. A nice woman at the library paid for me to print those out."

Clark sighed and closed his eyes.

"What's wrong?" Lily asked.

Clark bit his lip, he didn't know what to say. "Nothing. I'm just tired."

"Do you want to sleep here? I'm sure my aunt wouldn't mind if you slept on the couch."

Clark shook his head. Lily, the library, the drowned boy's bed, it was too much. He needed to be by himself. "You shouldn't be inviting strangers here when your aunt's away."

"My aunt and my mother don't like that rule about never talking to strangers. 'We're all strangers until we meet.' That's one of their sayings."

"They sound like I'd like them," said Clark.

"I think they'd like you," said Lily.

"Don't be too sure of that," said Clark. "I'm not usually a hit with mothers or aunts."

"My mother is not the usual mother," said Lily. "Neither is my aunt."

She lifted her chin, expecting Clark to kiss her. But he didn't. He closed the door without saying another word.

10

CLARK STRETCHED IN THE SAND, GRINDING THE SAND INTO HIS SKIN. It felt horrible. Sand was in every orifice. He spat out sand that had crusted around his mouth. He ran into the ocean, knowing it was the one chance he had of clearing his mood. The waves were rough and they tumbled him around. He caught one wave wrong and ended up jamming his head into the floor of the ocean. He scrambled up and with a roar hit the next wave chest high. When he walked out of the ocean, he felt cleaner, more ready.

He walked up the beach toward the Boardwalk. He didn't notice someone pause and follow him with her eyes. It was the volunteer Lily had met at the library. She patted her pocket and found Lily's flyer. She tossed it over the railing of the Boardwalk. The wind picked it up and it skittered over the sand. Clark stepped on it. He reached down, although normally he wouldn't have given the garbage that floated his way a second thought. But the "ghost writing" caught his eye. He picked it up and saw Lily's name. He glanced up at the Boardwalk. He saw the back of the woman from the library. Clark read the flyer carefully, which he hadn't in Lily's apartment. Her tour was gathering by the elephants at the Taj Mahal. He would be there. He would do what he could to protect Lily, even from herself.

Lily wasn't ready to sleep after Clark left. She wanted to talk to somebody about him. She considered calling her friend Bonnie, but the family Bonnie was staying with didn't like it when she got calls late at night.

At three in the morning she was still awake. She tried all her mother's tricks to bring on sleep; deep breathing, talking quietly to each body part, starting with her toes. Nothing worked. She kept rearranging the pillows, punching them up, then turning them over.

Finally, she turned on the light, hoping Aunt Andrea wouldn't see it. It wasn't just Clark. She was worried about what she would say on her tour. Could she really pull it off? She studied the notes that she had made. Everything she had written looked boring to her. Then she wrote down the words, *restless souls*. She tried for sleep one last time. She turned off the light and rearranged the pillows for the hundredth time. This time whatever she did worked. She slept.

In the morning Lily got up and took a shower. She looked at herself in the mirror. She expected to see circles under her eyes—but instead she looked wide awake. She felt terrific, almost tingling. She made a face at herself in the mirror, liking what she saw.

She enjoyed having her father's height. She had hated it in eighth grade when she had grown five

inches in a year. Then she had towered over most of
the boys, and her bones had ached. Back then, she
would gladly have traded several years of her life to
stop growing. She could remember lying in bed and
thinking, if it meant living to eighty instead of
eighty-four and not growing one more inch, she'd
make the deal. But the more she grew, the better she
got at soccer—both in quickness and in her ability to
see over the attacking team. Now she wouldn't have
traded her height for anything.

She picked up her notes, terrified that they would
make no sense. But she could make out her writing.
She was nervous, and wished she had time to practice
out loud. She straightened her shoulders and went
out with the sign she had made last night.

The weather was beautiful—a good omen. The sun
glistened on the waves. A breeze from the ocean kept
the Boardwalk cool. Lily stood impatiently next to
the white elephant, wondering if anyone would show
up. Finally an elderly lady, short and plump, wearing
a polka-dot dress that emphasized how round she
was, came up to her. The lady in polka dots gawked at
Lily's sign. "This looks interesting," she said.

"It will be," Lily promised.

From another direction Lily heard a "Yoo-hoo!" It
was June, bringing with her a group of about six. Lily
grinned at her. "I saw one of your flyers," shouted
June. "And I told all my friends that this was one side
of Atlantic City they couldn't miss."

"Thank you," said Lily, truly grateful. Six customers, plus the woman in polka dots. It was enough to start. She didn't notice at first that Clark had arrived. He watched her and said nothing. He stood with his arms folded over the back of his rolling chair, looking very much the way he had the day Lily met him.

"Will it really be good exercise?" said one overweight woman in a pink jogging suit.

The woman next to her looked downhearted. "I've got arthritis," she said. "I can't go so fast."

Clark moved forward. "At your service, ma'am," he said politely to the woman who was worried about her arthritis. "My chair comes free of charge with Lily's tour."

He winked at Lily and she relaxed. She took a deep breath. "Ladies and gentlemen," she began. Her voice came out surprisingly strong. "Let me take you on a journey to the past. We begin at the beginning. For centuries this island remained nearly uninhabited. The Absegami tribe walked the beach, they lit their campfires. Picture yourself as part of that tribe. You live in the piney woods by the ocean, the very woods that become a playground for the people who will destroy your tribe. You look out at the ocean through the flames of your fires. You know that your ancestors thirst for revenge. One day, you too will die. You will stay and haunt and torment those who think they can escape into their pleasure domes."

Clark watched her. Lily gestured with her arms, not in a parody of a Native American, but somehow evoking the spirits of the souls filled with a thirst for revenge.

"For centuries this island remained nearly uninhabited. But other restless souls walked its beaches. Pirates shipwrecked on the shoals just beyond the reef. Dead souls wandered here from the ships of the doomed Confederate navy as they tried to break the Union blockade. All those souls joined together patiently because the spirits knew that their time in the sun was coming. Then, a certain doctor enticed the railroad to come to this island at the total cost of 1,274,030 dollars, a lot of money in those days. He was a white man, Dr. Jonathan Pitney. Atlantic City was about to fulfill its wonderful and terrible curse—to become the home for restless souls."

Clark listened to her—her voice was pitched low—the timbre perfect. Lily had discovered the essence of Atlantic City—its curse—its everlasting restlessness.

"Come along with me," said Lily. "We will walk the Boardwalk of Dreams that can turn to nightmares—of promises that turn to curses."

She gestured up toward the glamorous Trump Taj. "Most of you have been inside the casino," she said. "And perhaps you were even greeted by the Donald, the man who considers himself Atlantic City's royalty."

Lily swept her hand out to the pier in front of the casinos. "Picture thousands of gaslights, twinkling merrily—competing with the stars of the sky—for here in the 1890s, the Steel Pier was the Showplace of the Nation. The Steel Pier was Atlantic City's crown jewel, but underneath lay tragedy. To entertain people, horses were made to dive into a tiny tub of water—sometimes breaking the back of the daredevil young girls who were fearless enough to ride them.

"Of course, it wasn't all tragedy," said Lily, thinking it was time for a little comic relief. "Here sat Billy and Benny, the world's largest twins. Imagine the sight of them. They used to have contests to see how many people could fit into one of their T-shirts. I think the record was forty."

Then Lily lowered her voice. "Let us go on. Millions of visitors came to parade on the Boardwalk—just as you do now—unaware that the curse of the restless souls would never leave this place or them in peace. Picture if you will, ladies in long dresses in their summer splendor, men in top hats. Suddenly a swarm of mosquitoes dive-bombed the grounds that we stand on today. So many mosquitoes swarmed the place that horses stampeded, causing carriage wrecks. One horse tipped over a kerosene lamp and the place went up in flames. Were they really mosquitoes?" Lily pitched her voice even lower. "Or were they restless souls seeking revenge?" Lily smiled a malevolent smile.

"I told you this would be exciting," said June to one of her friends.

Lily took a deep breath. Clark walked up beside her. "You're amazing at this. You're really good."

"Thanks," said Lily. "My palms are sweating."

"You've got everybody else's palms sweating too—where did you come up with that curse of the restless souls?" he asked. He tried to make his voice casual.

"It just came to me in the middle of the night," said Lily. She sounded almost giddy with excitement.

"This has been wonderful," said June as Lily concluded her tour. She handed Lily five dollars.

"I'd like to go again," said the woman in the polka-dot dress.

"I have plenty more to show you," said Lily. "Every tour will be different. We still haven't gotten to the drowned boy's bedroom."

Clark watched her. "Will you really take them there?" he asked, his voice full of wonder. Lily actually seemed to have no fear. She had sat on the drowned boy's bed and seemed unaffected in the morning. Could she possibly be the one to finally set him free? The thought of it made him dizzy.

"Come on," Lily said to Clark. "I'll buy you lunch with my earnings. My next tour isn't until two."

"No thanks," said Clark.

Lily looked puzzled. "Is anything wrong?" she asked.

"No. I just want to be alone."

"Do you want to bring your chair around for my second tour? I might have more people for you. You didn't have to do it for free—that was so nice." Lily tried to be convincing, tried to keep Clark around.

Clark shook his head. She watched him go, totally misunderstanding his reaction to her. Twice she had invited him to be with her, and twice he had rejected her. She sighed. "Guys," she muttered to herself. "Why do I even bother?"

CLARK LEFT LILY. He wandered into one of the casinos. He always found the casinos relaxing. Their noise never bothered him. He liked the artificial light, the constant zinging of the machines. Here the bright sunlight disappeared and one never knew whether it was day or night. Clark knew his way so well around the casinos that he could sneak into any swimming pool or entertainment lounge that he wished. He could make himself look older at will, and he could always pass for twenty-one. If he wanted to gamble, he could. But he wasn't looking for entertainment, he just needed time, time to think about what he was going to do about Lily.

If he let events take their course, she would be doomed. But it was within his power to save her. "Hey, buddy," said one of the blackjack dealers. "Do you want to play?"

Clark shook his head. "Not your game," he said.

Lily returned to her aunt's apartment just about dark. "How did your first tours go?" Aunt Andrea asked her.

"Fine," said Lily, "but the second tour felt flat compared to the first one, more like work." Lily laughed when she heard herself. "I know. It *is* work. I earned forty dollars."

"That's great, sweetie. That's way over minimum wage. You couldn't get a job that paid you that."

"Plus, it's fun," said Lily.

"There's a postcard from your mother," said Aunt Andrea.

"I didn't know they had postcards on vision quests," Lily muttered. She looked at the card from her mother. It was a painting of four coyotes howling at a moon. In the cradle of the moon sat a white dog looking very content to be just out of reach of the coyotes' jaws.

Lily's mother wrote, *You have the strength of the coyotes in your blood, their cunning and their wisdom. According to legends, coyotes love to play tricks, so watch that your sense of humor doesn't get you in trouble, but always remember to laugh. The moon of the desert shines on you too. So look at the moon and know I love you.*

"It doesn't exactly tell us much about her vacation," Lily said, showing the card to her aunt.

"Well, the drawing is beautiful," she said. "And your mom loves you."

"I wonder if she's got her new name yet?" Lily asked. "I hope she's not going to come back and ask me to call her Howls at Moon."

"Your mother means well." Andrea winced as she pulled off her shoes. "The worst thing about this job, is that the boss makes me wear high heels," she groaned. "I wish I would get that dealer's job. Dealers are allowed to wear comfortable shoes—even the female dealers. My feet are killing me."

"Here," said Lily. She helped Aunt Andrea swing her feet onto the couch. Lily rubbed them, slowly drawing her knuckles along the instep. Aunt Andrea sighed with satisfaction. "You give the best foot massages."

"I owe it to Mom," admitted Lily. "She studied foot reflexology. The Chinese believe that your feet are a map of your entire body. Mom thinks you can cure almost anything by applying pressure to the right part of your foot."

Lily rubbed under Aunt Andrea's big toe. Aunt Andrea winced. "That's where headaches live," said Lily. She rubbed more gently.

Aunt Andrea sighed. "Some man is going to be very lucky to get you. You're smart, pretty and you already know how to give happy feet."

Lily looked down at her aunt's swollen feet. Reggie had loved foot massages, but it wasn't enough to keep him from breaking up with her. After a hard soccer game, Lily's own feet could have used a rub. Reggie had never offered to massage her feet. Lily suspected that she could have rubbed his feet until doomsday, and he would still have said to her, "I think we're getting too involved." She wondered how Clark would like foot massages.

"Ouch!" said Aunt Andrea. Lily hadn't realized

that she had been digging her knuckles into the soft fleshy part of Andrea's heel.

"Sorry," said Lily. "I was just daydreaming."

The phone rang. "If it's for me, tell them I'm not here," said Aunt Andrea. "I'm too tired to talk to anybody."

Lily picked up the phone. "Bonnie!" She giggled. "Your timing's great. I've been wanting to talk to you. It's for me," she shouted to Aunt Andrea. Lily stretched the cord as far it could go and took the phone into the kitchen.

"So how are you doing?" Bonnie asked. "Met any wild gamblers?"

"No," said Lily. "I do have a scheme to get some spending cash from them, though. I'm giving a tour of the haunted Atlantic City. I know it sounds a little freaky, but Atlantic City is a very bizarre place."

"I can't believe I'm baby-sitting all summer, and you're earning money giving haunted tours. What a great idea!"

"Well, it kind of came to me on my first day. I met one of the chair pushers here. He's . . ." Lily hesitated.

"Chair pusher? What's that?"

Lily explained.

"So is he cute?" Bonnie asked.

Lily hesitated.

"Lily? Fess up."

"He's more than cute," she conceded.

"What does he look like?"

"He's tall, and he's got very nice eyes. And beautiful soft skin."

"Whoa! Soft skin. This sounds hot. So tell me, what's his hard luck story?"

"Bonnie!" protested Lily.

"Hey, this is me, remember. I know you never met a guy you didn't want to save. Let's see." Lily could visualize Bonnie counting her old boyfriends off on her fingers. "Clifton had dyslexia, and our fifth grade teachers were giving him a hard time. He was your first boyfriend."

"That was just a joke."

"Then there was Jeremiah. His parents were going through a nasty divorce. That was seventh grade."

"Eighth grade was Tom," Lily confessed. "He was suffering from a major depression because his dog had died."

"And finally, good old Reginald. His problem was a permanent case of a swelled head. "

Lily laughed.

"Just remember," warned Bonnie. "You're on the rebound."

"What's that supposed to mean?"

"Don't fall too hard or too soon," said Bonnie. "So what's this guy's problem?"

"Nothing," said Lily, refusing to tell Bonnie that Clark had run away from home because of an alcoholic mother. She could just imagine Bonnie's reaction. "He's sarcastic, that's the only problem I know."

"Sarcastic, that sounds promising. Reggie wouldn't have known a joke if he fell on it. If he's sarcastic, maybe he's smart."

"I think he is smart," said Lily.

"Good. Then he won't mind your sick sense of humor."

"Thank you very much. I don't think my sense of humor is sick."

"Okay—twisted. Is that better?"

"Yes," said Lily. "So tell me what's going on with you."

"What's going on with me? The woman that I'm 'au pairing' for thinks that I'm supposed to do the laundry and all the cleaning too. Plus, I'm supposed to help serve when they have dinner parties."

"Sounds like a blast!"

"It is. And, that jerk Daryl hasn't called all summer. Anyhow, let me know what happens with this guy. Does he have a name? Or do I have to keep calling him 'this guy'?"

"He's got a name," said Lily. "Clark."

"Clark? As in Clark Kent? Sounds sexy," said Bonnie.

"He is," admitted Lily. "But difficult. He gets close and then he runs away."

"So what else is new," said Bonnie. Lily laughed. She felt relieved. Somehow talking to Bonnie made everything with Clark seem so much more normal.

12

THE NEXT MORNING THE SKY LOOKED THREATENING. Thunderclouds piled up like mashed potatoes that hadn't been peeled—streaks of dark layered into the white. The wind was blowing off the ocean. Rain was definitely bad for Lily's business. She'd be lucky to get one customer in such bleak weather. She left her aunt's apartment, carrying her sign, feeling depressed.

As she turned the corner onto the Boardwalk, a gust of wind blew her hair around her face, like a halo. "You look good like that," said Clark. Lily swiveled around. It was embarrassing to have so much hair that sometimes it obstructed her vision. Clark's own brown hair was wet and slicked back as if he had just been swimming.

"A little cold to be swimming," Lily said. She kept her voice cool. She didn't want to sound eager after the way he had rebuffed her yesterday.

"The water's warmer than the air," said Clark. "How come I never see you in the water? Unless someone's drowning," he added, teasingly.

"It looks too stormy to swim," answered Lily.

"Are you kidding? It's the most fun to swim in a storm. The swells come in on you, and nobody else is out there." Clark looked at her. "Someday I'd like to teach you to swim."

"I never told you I couldn't swim," said Lily.

The wind picked up Lily's sign like a sail and almost knocked her over. "Here," said Clark. "Give it to me. I can hold it in the wind."

"So can I," Lily said.

Clark reached for the sign. His eyes were level with hers. He had a swimmer's body, a broad chest and slim hips. Today his green eyes looked grayish. His eyes seemed to change with the weather, reflecting the color of the ocean. Lily's dark brown eyes never changed.

"Look, I'm sorry for the way I was yesterday after your tour. I just took off. Sometimes I just get these moods. Nobody should have to be around me when I'm like that. I should have said thank you when you invited me to lunch. I screwed up. I'm sorry."

"Those are magic words," she said.

"Which? I'm sorry or I screwed up."

"Both," laughed Lily. Clark wasn't afraid to say I'm sorry. She couldn't remember Reggie ever saying he was sorry, much less meaning it. Reggie's face had been hard to read, but Clark didn't seem to mind that every thought in his head flashed out from his eyes.

"Truce," he said. "I'll carry your sign."

"I don't know if anyone will come." Just then one of the casino doors opened and a group of about three tourists spotted the sign.

"Oh good, she's here," said the woman. Lily recognized her as the one who had been wearing the polka-dot dress yesterday. Today she was dressed in lime green. "I know you'll enjoy this," she said to her friends. "It was such fun. And the tour guide said it would be different each time."

"Oh yes," Lily improvised. She really had lied about that. She hadn't figured on people taking the tour twice in a row. "Today is a perfect day for the drowned boy's bedroom. A bedroom sits on a lawn, right next to the Boardwalk, and it never gets wet."

Lily led her group past the casinos toward the drowned boy's bed. "I will tell you a tragic story of a mother's grief and the power of the ocean. The boy was the son of Kitty Gurney, one of the wealthiest women in town."

"I read about her in a magazine they left in our hotel room," said one woman. "Mrs. Gurney is supposed to have a fabulous art collection."

"She's a great patron of the arts," said Lily. "She donates to the hospital and to all the charities. Some people say that she is the heart and soul of Atlantic City. But remember, you are standing on the Boardwalk of the city of troubled souls." Lily's tour looked down at their feet as if they expected to see fiendish souls rising up from under the boards.

As they left the casinos, Lily continued her story. "The Gurney boy drowned tragically. His mother could never forgive herself or the ocean that took her son. She had his bed placed on the lawn, so that he would know to come home. The bed is like a beacon. Naturally, the neighbors did not approve. We're going to be walking past some of the most expensive homes in Atlantic City. Some of her neighbors protested. But she refused to move the bed. It just sits on the lawn, waiting for Mrs. Gurney's son to return, and it stays as dry as a bone."

Clark could see how much Lily was enjoying herself. Her group was salivating at the details. They were like those fools he used to see on Halloween night on the Boardwalk. Adults taking what used to be a children's night and making it their own, dressing up in outlandish costumes—giving themselves one more excuse to cut loose. He gazed out at the waves. He could tell a storm was coming.

They were at the edge of the commercial part of the Boardwalk. Clark glanced up. The young fortune-teller was walking a little terrier. She waved at Lily and Clark, but Lily was so entranced by what she was doing, she didn't notice her. Clark gave the fortune-teller a halfhearted wave. She put her hand up to her mouth as if to ward off evil.

Clark heard thunder in the distance. He didn't think Lily even heard the thunder. She was so intent on her tour. She led her group farther away from the casinos. Clark followed, carrying Lily's sign. "Gather around," Lily said as they reached the Cannon mansion. "There is a second tragedy I want to tell you about. It happened right in this house. A boy named Jimmy loved to play in the waves." She told the story of how Jimmy's parents had objected to Mrs. Gurney placing her son's bed on the lawn.

There was another low rumble of thunder in the distance.

"And now," said Lily. "Let's get a closer look at the bed. A little rain won't hurt us." Lily led them to the railing in front of the Gurney red brick house. In the gray light of the storm, the house looked snug and warm. The yellow lights from the windows gave out a warming glow.

"Oh, what lovely flowers," cooed one woman. "Does someone still live in this house?"

"Yes," said Lily. "Mrs. Gurney lives here today. That's why the bedroom is still out on the lawn."

"I hope she changes the sheets," joked one older woman.

"She must have loved her son very much," said the one gentleman on the tour. Clark gave the bed a fixed look. All mothers didn't love their sons, he thought to himself. Mothers could pretend to love, but love could be a mask for ownership. A mother who refused to let her son go was not a loving mother.

"Tell us more about the bed," urged one of the women. Lily glanced at Clark. He had an odd expression on his face. But she didn't have time for him right now. She turned to her group, pointing at the bed, dramatically. "The bed is waiting, waiting for the boy to come to his final resting place."

"His body was never found?" asked one of the women.

"Never," answered Lily.

The group edged forward until they were all leaning against the Boardwalk railing, some standing on the rail to get a better view. "The poor mother truly must have been heartbroken," said one woman.

"I wouldn't want to sleep out there—mosquitoes," said an elderly man. "I always hated camping."

"It's not camping," said the lady in lime green. "The boy's dead. You can't go camping if you're dead."

Clark stood beside Lily, looking down at the bed. She touched him on the arm. "Are you all right?" she asked. "Does the bed depress you?" Lily asked.

Clark laughed. Lily wondered if it was because his own mother hadn't even seemed to mind when he had moved out as a child. Suddenly she felt a wet drop on her arm. It was raining. Shaded by the tree, the bed seemed dry.

"Maybe you should get your group out of the rain," warned Clark.

"They came prepared," said Lily. Like characters in a cartoon, one by one, each brought out a folding umbrella and popped it open against the rain. In addition, most of the women took a little pleated plastic rain bonnet out of their purses. "My group makes the Boy Scouts look like unprepared amateurs," said Lily.

"I want to see if the bed is really dry," said one of the women. She flung her umbrella over the Boardwalk. "Whoops," she said gleefully, "my umbrella fell onto the lawn." The driveway had turned from gray to black as the drops covered the asphalt.

"I bet there's a clear plastic box around it," said the elderly gentleman. "A good one. You can't see the edges."

"I don't see a box," said one woman.

"Maybe she's got it covered in Saran Wrap," said another.

Lily touched Clark's shoulder. "Clark, tell me what's wrong?"

Clark looked at her. "Why do you think something is wrong?" he asked.

"I don't know," admitted Lily. "But I know this bed scares you."

"And it doesn't scare you?" Clark asked.

Lily shook her head. She remembered that night when she had been mesmerized by the bed and had sat on it. "No," she said. "For some reason I am fascinated by this bed."

Clark stared at her. "Oh, Lily," he moaned. "It's a terrible choice. And one of us is going to have to make it."

"I don't understand. What choice?"

Before Clark could answer, Lily heard someone call her name. She turned toward the voice, and she didn't see the look of horror cross Clark's face.

THE DOOR TO MRS. GURNEY'S HOUSE OPENED. Lily's tour group scurried behind her as if they wanted to be sure she was the one who would catch the blame for trespassing. To Lily's shock it was the woman from the library walking briskly across the lawn, wearing high-heeled pumps. Her shoes left little holes in the lawn. "Lily," she shouted.

Lily couldn't believe that she could have missed the resemblance between the woman in the library and the old photographs of Mrs. Gurney. The years hadn't diminished her beauty.

"I'm so sorry, Mrs. Gurney," Lily said quickly. "We didn't mean to intrude. The wind picked up an umbrella and it fell on your lawn."

Mrs. Gurney stooped and picked up the umbrella. The woman who had dropped it took it from her gingerly. Mrs. Gurney smiled. "The wind can be so careless of possessions," she said. Mrs. Gurney was perfectly made up, her lipstick bright red against the papery paleness of her thin cheeks. She was wearing a black knit dress suit with a bright red silk blouse underneath.

"Lily, this must be your tour." She nodded to the group. She spoke as if she were the queen of England greeting her subjects.

Lily gestured vaguely toward the bed. "I didn't realize that you were Mrs. Gurney. I didn't know."

"I prefer to volunteer at the library anonymously," said Mrs. Gurney. "You know, when I saw the flyer in the library, I wondered if you had included my house. Of course, I didn't want to suggest it."

Lily stared at her. Could Mrs. Gurney mean it? She really wanted her house on a tour of the weird and horrible sights of Atlantic City? Then Lily remembered the floodlights that lit up the bed at night. Mrs. Gurney wasn't afraid of tourists' curiosity. Clearly there was something in her that almost sought the publicity.

Rain came down in a fine mist. Mrs. Gurney glanced up at the sky. "Let's not stand around in the rain. Why don't you and your group come in for some tea?"

Clark was in Lily's peripheral vision. He shook his head vigorously. "We wouldn't want to impose," said Lily.

The woman who had dropped the umbrella interrupted. "It is getting chilly, and we would so love to see your beautiful house."

"Come in," insisted Mrs. Gurney. Lily's tour trooped into the house. Lily and Clark were the last in line. The rain was coming down harder now. The pillows and sheet on the bed seemed dry. The wind whipped Lily's hair around, but the blanket on the bed didn't even rustle. Clark shivered. He thought of bones lying on the bottom of the ocean. He didn't want to go into the house, but he didn't want to let Lily go in without him.

"You don't have to go in, you know," said Clark.

"I've got to go in," said Lily. "My tour's in there."

"Don't" persisted Clark.

"I have to," insisted Lily.

Clark realized this might be the last choice she would make. He followed her into the house.

In the foyer Mrs. Gurney took their umbrellas and rain gear. Then she ushered them into her living room. It was very large, yet cozy. Four comfortable couches upholstered in a print of big cabbage roses dominated the room. In one corner was a baby grand piano, covered with a lace shawl. Track lighting hung from the ceiling, and there were many paintings on the wall, each spotlit by a light from the ceiling. Sliding glass doors looked out over the ocean. The rain was coming down heavier now, splattering the glass doors. Fog coming up from the ocean obscured the view of the bed on the lawn.

Mrs. Gurney drew the drapes halfway. "There, that's more restful," she said. The drapes also had big cabbage roses on them. They matched the print on the couches, somehow making the huge room slightly claustrophobic. After closing the drapes, Mrs. Gurney took Lily's arm and led her to one of the couches. An ivory and ebony chess set sat on the coffee table, its pieces lined up as if ready for a game.

"So," said Mrs. Gurney, addressing Lily's tour. "You've come to see a side of Atlantic City that most tourists miss."

"Lily seems so knowledgeable for a girl so young," said the woman in lime green.

"That's because she's industrious. Aren't you, dear?"

Lily searched Mrs. Gurney's eyes for a hint of ridicule, but she didn't find any.

Clark sat on a couch opposite Lily, slouched in it, his long legs stretching out into the middle of the room. "Young man, I don't believe we've been introduced."

Clark stood up, holding his hand out politely. "Clark DeLuge, ma'am," he said softly.

Mrs. Gurney took his hand. "DeLuge, it's an unusual name."

"Yes, ma'am," said Clark. "But as Shakespeare said, 'Tis an ill-favored thing, but mine own.'"

"Do you often quote Shakespeare?" asked Mrs. Gurney. "It tells me that you had a good upbringing. Perhaps you owe your love of Shakespeare to your mother."

"If you remember Hamlet, Shakespeare wasn't too fond of mothers."

"I always felt Gertrude was misunderstood," said Mrs. Gurney. She chortled. The pearls around her neck bobbed. She turned to Lily's group. "Teenagers today take themselves so seriously, don't they? I think they should relax more."

Lily's group all nodded their heads as if they agreed with Mrs. Gurney. Clark watched them carefully. He had the feeling that if Mrs. Gurney had said the moon was pink, they would have agreed with her.

Lily unclasped her hands and rubbed them on her black jeans. All during Clark's banter with Mrs. Gurney she had felt nervous. Her hands felt clammy. She tried to sit back on the cushions. The down in the pillows of the couch was so thick that she felt like she was falling into a deep snowbank.

"I'll see to the tea," said Mrs. Gurney. She walked out of the room. She strode with the grace of a dancer.

"Oh, this is so exciting," said the woman who had dropped the umbrella. "Wait till we tell the others on our bus that we were invited into this house. They'll be so jealous."

"Isn't this house magnificent?" said the woman in lime green. "And her jewels. Did you see that diamond on her finger?"

"I just know that suit is a Chanel," said her friend, "but I think she wears too much makeup."

"I don't know," said the one elderly gentleman. "I think she's a fine-looking lady."

"Maybe you should try dating her," said Clark with a grin. He stood up and stretched. He walked to the couch where Lily was sitting. He plunked down next to her. "You could drown in these pillows," he said.

"I'm not sure you should mention drowning in this house," Lily warned.

"You worried she's got the place bugged?" Clark asked. "She obviously loves the publicity. You should have made her the star attraction of your tour."

"It is strange—I thought she'd be more private. A friend of my aunt's told me that Mrs. Gurney hasn't allowed her picture to be taken since her son died."

"Vanity," said Clark. "She probably doesn't like people to see that she's actually gotten older."

"She's still beautiful."

Clark looked thoughtful. "I suppose she is," he admitted.

Lily's tour members had spread out around the living room, looking at the different paintings and portraits. "These paintings are gorgeous," said the lady in lime green. "I just know that's an Impressionist masterpiece."

"It's a Monet, one of his small watercolors from his garden in Giverny," said Mrs. Gurney, coming into the room, pushing a cart with gold wheels. "I find it soothing."

"She owns a Monet," Lily whispered to Clark. "We studied him in art class. That painting must be worth a fortune."

Mrs. Gurney poured out a cup of tea and handed the first cup to Lily. The cup and saucer were of such delicate china that Lily was afraid she'd break it. Her fingers felt too large for the handle. Lily took a sip of the tea. It scalded the roof of her mouth.

She put down the cup. "Let me help you serve the others," she said. She pushed herself up from the couch.

Mrs. Gurney smiled at her indulgently. "Thank you. I can't abide servants in the house. I haven't been able to stand anyone living here since my son died." Lily didn't know what to say. She served all her tour members. Then she handed a cup of tea to Clark. He took it, sticking his pinkie high in the air as he sipped. Lily sat next to him. She picked up her cup. The tea had cooled somewhat; the woodsy flavor was delicious.

Mrs. Gurney started to pour herself a cup. "Let me help you, ma'am," said Clark. He leaped up to hold the teacup for Mrs. Gurney while she poured. The cup was several inches from the spout.

"You're holding the cup at an awkward angle," Mrs. Gurney warned Clark. "I could burn you."

"Once burned, once warned," said Clark. "Even a cat who steps on a hot burner learns to avoid the stove." He righted the cup.

"Ah, but cats have nine lives. How many do you have?" asked Mrs. Gurney. Lily listened to the two of them. If she hadn't known Mrs. Gurney was so old, she would have sworn she was flirting with Clark.

Lily sipped her tea. Her head sank back on the pillows. A wave of exhaustion hit her. In biology class after lunch sometimes her head would jerk back, and she would realize that she had nodded off. She listened to the voices of the old ladies and men drift over her and felt she was back in class. Her tour group was complimenting Mrs. Gurney on her artworks. Lily looked around. It was a hodgepodge collection— all different styles; although many were beautiful, some were quite strange.

"You have such unusual taste," exclaimed one woman. She had stopped in front of a modern painting that was all angles and bright orange colors.

Lily glanced at the painting. It gave her a headache.

"That's a portrait of my son," said Mrs. Gurney.

The woman jumped back a little, as if she had touched one of the buzzers in the arcade on the Boardwalk that gave off little shocks.

"I painted that myself. I studied with some of the modern masters when I was a girl."

"Personally, I like the old style better," said the old man.

"Yes, they are more soothing," said Mrs. Gurney. She made the word "soothing" sound like a put-down.

"You have many portraits here," said the elderly gentleman, standing in front of a teenage girl gazing romantically out at the ocean with her toes in the water.

Clark looked at the painting. "It's a little too sweet for my taste."

"Ah, you have good taste," said Mrs. Gurney. "That is one of my least favorites." She seemed to be sharing a joke with herself.

"Too much gauzy blues and grays," asserted Clark.

Mrs. Gurney studied the painting. "You know, young man, you are exactly right. You might have an untrained eye, but you have definite taste. It needed stronger colors."

Lily tried to focus on the painting they were looking at, but the colors ran together in her head. She wanted to take a closer look. She tried to get up, but the soft pillows felt as if they were grabbing at her.

"Do you need a hand?" asked Clark. He stood over her, giving her a smile.

"Yes," she said. "I swear this couch is made of Velcro."

"Lily, dear, you don't look well," said Mrs. Gurney.

"Alley-oop," said Clark, leaning back and pulling her up off the couch. Lily staggered. Her knees buckled. Bile from her stomach rose in her throat. She put her hand to her mouth, afraid that she was going to throw up all over the couch.

"Lily?" Clark's voice sounded anxious. Lily sank back down on the couch.

Mrs. Gurney hustled over and pushed Clark aside to look at Lily. "You look positively green," exclaimed Mrs. Gurney. Lily had the feeling that Mrs. Gurney was upset that she clashed with the roses on the couch. The tour group gathered around. Lily could see the lime green pants, and she felt sick to her stomach all over again.

"I'm okay," she managed to gasp out. She wanted them all to move away and give her air, but they just came closer, patting her on the shoulder, looking concerned. Mrs. Gurney sat on the couch beside Lily. "My dear," she asked, "what's wrong?"

Sweat was pouring down Lily's neck and back. She was clammy all over. "I'm fine," she said, trying to smile. "Something just came over me." Lily's arms and legs were tingling. She felt really sick. She knew she'd never be able to walk back to the casinos. "Could you get a cab for us? I'll take my group down to the casinos and go home."

Mrs. Gurney patted her hand. "Of course, dear," she said. "You look like you've got a fever."

"Maybe she shouldn't go home alone," suggested one of the women.

A quiver shook Lily's body. Her shoulders shuddered. She couldn't stop quaking. Mrs. Gurney put a shawl over her shoulders. "You *are* too sick to go home alone," she said. "Give me a number to call."

"You look awful," Clark said to Lily.

"It's 555–8760. But, please, don't worry my aunt. Tell her that it's just a little flu. The other night at dinner, something like this came over me."

Mrs. Gurney left the room to make the telephone calls. Clark took a cloth napkin from the tea service and wiped the sweat off her face.

"I'm sweating like a pig. I don't know what came over me. I'll be better when I get some fresh air."

"Won't we all?" whispered Clark.

Lily wanted to tell him something important, but she couldn't think of what it was. "Clark . . ." Her tongue felt twice its normal size, filling her mouth. Mrs. Gurney came back into the room. "The taxis will be here in a moment," she said.

"Oh, thank goodness," said the woman in lime green who insisted on hovering over Lily. "Lily should be where she can be taken care of. She is looking terrible."

"She seems to be getting worse," said the elderly man.

"Oh, dear," said Mrs. Gurney, "no one was home at her aunt's house. I was going to just let her go with you. But perhaps I shouldn't."

"I can take her to her aunt's house," said Clark. "I've been there before. I know where it is."

Mrs. Gurney looked him up and down. "I think perhaps she is too sick to travel."

"I'll take care of her," said Clark. "I'm leaving with her."

Lily struggled to rise again from the couch. "I'll be fine." But once she was standing, she burst into tears. She was so embarrassed. She couldn't believe it. She was a person who rarely cried. "It's all right," said Mrs. Gurney, putting her thin arms around her, and lowering Lily to the couch. "You don't need to be afraid." Mrs. Gurney looked at Clark. "You can see, she's in no state to leave. The rest of you all had better go. Your taxis are waiting. I'll see you to the door."

Rain drummed on the windows. Lily tried to

struggle to her feet, but she felt again as if she was
going to vomit. Her head sank back against the flowered cushions of the couch. Through the half-pulled
drapes, she could see the bed. Although it was raining
harder, the mist and fog had lifted. The bed sat on the
lawn, its pillows plumped up. It was bone-dry.

Lily wiped her cheeks. They were soaked.

THROUGH SLITS IN HER EYES, LILY WATCHED CLARK. His lips were pulled down in a frown. "I don't want to leave you alone with her," he said softly. He reached down and touched her cheek with the palm of his hand. He turned her head toward him. He wiped a tear from her cheek. "Careful you don't drown in your tears," he said softly. When Lily had the flu her mother would tell her to just let moods pass over her. "The flu is your body's way of telling you to let go— that you need to rest. Don't make your body a battle-ground."

High heels made a clicking sound on the hard-wood floor between the oriental carpets. Mrs. Gurney returned to the room. She sat on the couch and put her hand on Lily's forehead. Her hand felt cool to the touch. Lily could smell the slight odor of roses from Mrs. Gurney's hand lotion. Mrs. Gurney turned to Clark. "I thought you had left with the others."

Clark hesitated. He looked around the room. "I'm going to stay with Lily," he said decisively.

"It's your choice," said Mrs. Gurney softly. Lily tried to lift her head. "She's burning up. I think she'll be better off in bed. Could you help me get her upstairs to the guest room? Take her to the room at the top of the stairs. It's the one with the stained glass window. I'll go call the doctor. I do wish I could have reached her aunt."

"I don't mean to be a bother," whispered Lily.

"You're not, dear," said Mrs. Gurney. Lily jerked her head. She could have sworn that she heard Mrs. Gurney say "You're not dead."

"What did you say?" Lily demanded in a suddenly strong voice.

"She said you wouldn't be a bother." Clark was looking at her strangely.

"I thought I heard something else," Lily mumbled. She tried to take a deep breath. She wasn't hearing right. She wasn't seeing right. Her body was out of control. She wanted to stay calm, but she was terrified.

She tried to push up from the couch. Clark put his arm around her waist. His chin was just above her shoulder.

There was a skylight over the stairwell, and Lily could hear rain tapping on it. She glanced up at the skylight. The rain sounded so loud. It pounded in her head, a booming sound that vibrated in her stomach, making her ill. "I wish the rain would stop," Lily whispered to Clark.

"It's getting lighter," said Clark.

The rain sounded torrential to her. "It sounds like a drum solo at a bad rock concert," she complained.

"What?" Clark asked.

"The rain . . . it's so loud."

"Lily, it's just a soft rainfall."

Lily shivered. She tried to support herself. Her legs weren't working right. Her knees were stiff. She had to mentally kick out at the ankle in order to make them go up the steps. Each step was agonizingly slow. Clark was patient with her. At the top of the stairs, he opened a door into a room dominated by a big bed with pillows and a twig headboard and footboard. Different colored ribbons were woven through the twigs. There were so many pillows on the bed, it didn't seem that there would be room for Lily.

"This room is freezing," Lily complained. Her teeth were chattering. Clark swept some of the pillows aside and lowered Lily onto the bed. He took a pink comforter from the foot of the bed and put it over her. "Is that better?" he asked.

Lily nodded, trying to get warm. "I don't know what's wrong with me."

"I wish I could tell you," said Clark. "I've never seen anybody get sick so fast. This room is hot, and you're freezing."

"It's not my fault," Lily said defensively.

Clark touched her face. "I didn't say it was, did I?"

Lily swallowed. It was hard to swallow. Clark pulled a chair close to the bed. "You look like you're auditioning for the Bride of Frankenstein—all pale and ghostly." He laughed. "You promised on your flyer that you'd offer thrills and chills—you can't be accused of false advertising."

"I wasn't planning on supplying the chills myself," said Lily. She tried to sit up. "I need a drink of water."

"Okay, sweetie, I'll get it for you," said Clark. He left the room.

"Sweetie." Her aunt called her "sweetie" or "honey" all the time. Reggie had never called her that or anything resembling an endearment. She tried to curl into a ball to get warm. She could vaguely make out flowered wallpaper but all the colors in the room ran together, looking muddy.

The light in the room was dusky, neither dark nor light. She shivered. She was chilled, and yet she couldn't stop sweating. She put her hand on her forehead. She tried to guess how high her temperature was. When she got the flu, she always liked to know her temperature. It made her feel that the illness was real.

Clark came back into the room, a glass of water in his hand. She fumbled as she grabbed for it and water spilled on the flowered quilt. For a second, Lily panicked.

"Here," said Clark. He took out his handkerchief and wiped up the spill. Lily remembered the handkerchief from the time they had rescued Jimmy. Lily took a sip. She glanced around the room and realized why the light had felt so strange. The one large window in the room was covered in stained glass—a beach scene, with a seagull flying over the waves.

"That window is beautiful," she said almost breathlessly.

Clark looked at it. "It makes me feel claustrophobic."

Lily looked around some more. The room was decorated within an inch of its life. Wallpaper of climbing roses covered three walls and the ceiling.

"Mrs. Gurney must love roses," said Lily. But the more she looked at the roses, the more she began to sweat. She saw thorns growing out of the wallpaper.

"The thorns," she whimpered.

Clark looked baffled. "Thorns?"

Lily nodded. "On the wallpaper."

"The wallpaper doesn't have real thorns. They're just painted on." Clark rubbed his thumb against the wallpaper. "See. No blood. No thorns. You're just hallucinating." He said it as if hallucinating was the most natural thing in the world. He propped a pillow behind her back.

Lily shivered. She sobbed out the word "thorn" again.

"No thorns, Lily," Clark said gently. He touched her shoulder. Lily clenched her eyes closed. She wouldn't look at the wallpaper.

"Your shirt is soaked," Clark said, rubbing his hand down her back.

"I know. I can't stop sweating."

Clark opened one of the dresser drawers. "Mrs. Gurney might not want you to go through her drawers," Lily warned.

Clark ignored her. "Here's a T-shirt," he said, pulling out an old gray T-shirt with nothing written on it. It looked big.

"Put it on," he said.

He turned his back on Lily and pretended to study the stained glass window. He could stand with his back to her and still see her in the mirror of the dresser. Maybe it was unfair of him to take advantage of the fact that she was sick, but he couldn't look away. She took off her shirt and unhooked her bra. He looked at her breasts and felt himself get excited. It was a powerful feeling—one that he enjoyed. It proved to him that even in this house, he could feel alive. He felt guilty too, but not guilty enough to stop.

Lily's shirt felt so clammy it was a relief to get her clothes off. She pulled the T-shirt over her head without embarrassment. The cloth was incredibly soft and worn.

"Can I turn around?" Clark asked.

"Yes."

"You look better," he said.

He bent down and unexpectedly kissed her neck, just at the edge of the T-shirt. "Oh, Lily," he said, sounding sad.

Lily shivered. "Are you still cold?" he asked, his voice low, whispering in her ear. He stretched out on the bed. He didn't press against her. He crossed his legs and looked out at the stained glass window. "Wouldn't you rather see the real sky?" he asked.

Lily was aware of all the things they weren't talking about—the kiss, her illness, the strange fact that they were inside the drowned boy's house. All that seemed off-limits. Instead they talked of interior decorating.

"I think the window is beautiful," she said.

Clark stroked her hair. "I think *you're* beautiful." He said it so softly Lily wasn't sure she had really heard the words. He stroked her forearm. It tickled. She tried to stay awake, but she couldn't. Her eyes closed. She couldn't have opened them if she tried. The world disappeared and she was groggy with sleep.

Clark watched Lily drowse. Once Clark had a dog who was sick, and he lay with the dog in his arms, constantly wanting to check if it was alive. Lily would be furious that he had compared her to a dog.

She stirred in her sleep. She seemed uncomfortable. Clark held her tighter. Then he felt his own eyes begin to close. Under the Boardwalk, he rarely slept for more than a few minutes at a time. But he knew that it was his choice to sleep under the Boardwalk, not to sleep in his mother's house. With Lily, he felt safer than he had in years. He laughed at himself. How ironic for someone like him to talk about being safe. The word didn't apply to him. It was even more ironic that he of all people should want to keep Lily safe. After all, he had put her in jeopardy in the first place. But now, watching her sleep, he wanted to continue to protect her, forever.

Lily's eyes snapped open. Everything was fuzzy. Mrs. Gurney stood over the bed. She was looking at them both with a rather amused expression on her face. Lily tried to sit up and talk, but her tongue had grown thick again. Mrs. Gurney sat on the edge of the bed next to Clark. "What is she saying?" she asked Clark.

Clark couldn't make out Lily's words. Lily waved her hands about. The thorns on the wallpaper seemed to be reaching out for her. "She seems upset about something," said Mrs. Gurney.

Lily began to choke. Mrs. Gurney handed Lily a ceramic mug with roses climbing all over it. The roses squirmed in Lily's vision. She tried to get her hand around the cup, but she couldn't seem to hold on to it. Mrs. Gurney held the cup up to Lily's lips. She swallowed. Her tongue felt like it was getting thicker and thicker.

Lily put her hand to her cheek. Her skin felt papery and dry. Mrs. Gurney gently pulled Lily's hand away from her face. "I've called the doctor," she said to Clark. "He's coming soon. I think she needs peace and quiet."

"He . . . he . . . " Lily tried to tell Mrs. Gurney that she wanted Clark to stay.

"Something has her upset," said Mrs. Gurney. "Let's leave her alone for a while. Maybe she'll sleep."

Lily pounded her hand on the comforter. She didn't want to be alone. "Clark!" Lily called out, but the only sound that came out was "Cl . . . uh . . . "

The sweats started again. "Rest, rest, dear," crooned Mrs. Gurney. She forced Lily's face into her chest and started to rock her back and forth. There was nothing soft to rest on. Her chest was bony. She rocked Lily jerkily. Lily's head bounced up and down on her chest. She tried to pull away. Mrs. Gurney's gold pin dug into Lily's cheek. The smell of Mrs. Gurney's rose perfume made her gag. She took a breath, struggling for air. With an unexpectedly abrupt movement, Mrs. Gurney stood up, letting Lily go. Lily's head banged against the twig bedpost.

"She should be alone," Mrs. Gurney said softly to Clark. "I'll talk to you outside." Mrs. Gurney walked out of the room. Clark followed her. The door closed behind them. Lily could hear Clark's voice. He didn't sound like himself. He was pleading, almost begging. Then the voices grew muffled. Lily could hear nothing except the ocean meeting the shore and then retreating. People paid good money for machines that could duplicate the sounds of the shore. It was supposed to be soothing, but to Lily's ears, the ocean sounded relentless.

LILY WOKE UP DRENCHED IN SWEAT. She had soaked through the T-shirt. Even the sheets were wet and clammy. She kicked at the sheets. Someone had made the bed with hospital corners so tight that she could barely turn.

She squinted at the stained glass window. Bright sunlight fractured the colors—the turquoises looked bright green, and the bird's red eye shone like a ruby. Her lips felt dry and cracked. She licked them. The ceramic mug with roses was still on the nightstand. She took a sip of the water, but it didn't taste good. There was a cup of stale tea next to the mug. Even though it was lukewarm, it tasted better than the water.

Lily rubbed her neck, wondering how long she had been sleeping. She heard a phone ring somewhere in the house. There was no phone in her room. Putting her teacup down, she kicked at the sheet and swung her legs out of bed.

She stood up and reeled. She took a deep breath. She hated the sweats. The room felt stifling. She grabbed the bedpost for support. Pushing against the wall, she stumbled over to the stained glass window. She pressed her cheek against the glass. It felt cool and bumpy. She pushed at the window. It slipped up on the sash easily.

The air felt damp and humid, not fresh. When she looked down, the boy's bed was on the lawn, directly under her window. Her stomach heaved. Just then the door opened, and Mrs. Gurney walked into the room. "Lily, you mustn't get out of bed. Come away from the window. Don't you remember the doctor told you to stay in bed?"

Lily stared at her. "What?"

Mrs. Gurney grabbed Lily around the waist and half pushed her away from the window toward the bed. "The doctor said you mustn't get out of bed until you're stronger."

"What doctor?" Lily's voice was hoarse—it sounded as if she hadn't used it for days.

"What doctor?" Lily repeated, forcing the words out. She had no memory of seeing any doctor.

Mrs. Gurney was looking at her warily. "The doctor said it was very important that you drink fluids to replace the ones that you're losing when you sweat at night."

Lily swallowed hard. Was Mrs. Gurney insane? Lily knew that she had not seen a doctor. "I never saw any doctor."

"You can't remember seeing the doctor?" Mrs. Gurney looked concerned. She sighed. "Have some tea."

"I want to go home," said Lily. "I want my aunt. I want my mother! My aunt must be frantic."

"Your aunt's been called. We all want you to go

home." Mrs. Gurney patted the pillows and fluffed them up around Lily. "You're soaked."

Lily fought to keep her breath calm. She practiced breathing through her nose, the way her mother had taught her in yoga—in out—in out.

"I have a nightgown for you," said Mrs. Gurney. "It's so much nicer than that old T-shirt." She handed Lily a soft cotton nightgown with tiny roses on it. On the front was a yoke of beautiful lace. She placed it on the covers.

"This is too beautiful for me," Lily said. "I'll sweat right through it."

"Nonsense. It will feel good. I'll help you change."

"I can do it myself."

"You're weak," said Mrs. Gurney. She took Lily's hands in hers. Mrs. Gurney's arms were strong. She held Lily's wrists above her head. Lily struggled.

"My dear," said Mrs. Gurney calmly. "I'm just try-ing to help." Her eyes were level to Lily's. Holding Lily's wrists above her head, Mrs. Gurney took both of Lily's hands in one of hers and with the other hand deftly stripped the T-shirt over Lily's head. She threw the T-shirt into a corner, letting go of Lily's hands. Lily pulled the nightgown on and shrunk back into the headboard—the twigs dug into her back. She crossed her arms over her breasts.

Mrs. Gurney smiled at her condescendingly. She poured a cup of tea and handed it to Lily. Lily tried to raise it to her lips. Her hand began to shake. Mrs. Gurney held the cup for her. "Lily dear, you know, in these three days, I feel I've come to know you—even though you've been asleep most of the time."

Lily dropped the teacup onto the bed. Tea dribbled down the front of her nightgown. "Three days!" she shrieked. Mrs. Gurney rescued the teacup. Lily reached for the handkerchief she didn't realize she had hidden under her pillow. She used it to blot up the spilled tea.

"You'll ruin that lovely handkerchief," said Mrs. Gurney. "Tannin from tea stains." She tried to pry the handkerchief from Lily's hand.

"It's mine!" said Lily fiercely, remembering that it was Clark's. It was the only thing of his that she had.

Mrs. Gurney smiled at her, and with that smile, Lily became powerless. Mrs. Gurney took the handkerchief. She smoothed it out. "What lovely embroidery," she said. Lily didn't remember the embroidery.

"Here," said Mrs. Gurney, returning the handkerchief. "It obviously means a lot to you. Although how strange . . . "

"What's strange?" asked Lily.

"Oh, nothing," said Mrs. Gurney. Lily looked at the embroidery. The stitching was in such elaborate gothic it was hard to read.

"You're lying about the doctor," said Lily, tucking the handkerchief back under the pillow.

"Lily, why would I lie to you?"

Lily's entire body shuddered. She pulled the cover to her chin. "It's not three days. It's not."

"You've been sleeping much of the time, which is

good. You need sleep. The doctor has been running some tests. At first he thought it could be chronic fatigue syndrome, but it usually doesn't come on so fast."

"My aunt! She probably called the police. How could you have kept me here without letting her know?"

Mrs. Gurney crossed her arms over her chest. She gave Lily a careful look, the way you do to a crazy person on the street. "Just seconds ago I told you that your aunt knows you're here. She came to see you yesterday. You talked to her. You saw her. Don't you remember? Your aunt is a lovely person. She talked to the doctor. I didn't want the responsibility of caring for you, but your aunt was beside herself. She couldn't take time off from work to care for you. This bedroom is unused. I offered to let you stay here."

Lily couldn't listen anymore. She pulled the covers up over her ears. "I'm going home."

Mrs. Gurney stood up. "I'll call your aunt at the casino. You can talk to her. Or, better yet, I'll see if I can get her to come here."

"Call her now!" Lily insisted.

Mrs. Gurney nodded. "I will," she said. There was steel in her voice. She left the room.

Lily stared at the stained glass window, realizing that Mrs. Gurney must have closed it. The seagull's ruby red eye was glaring at her. The red eye that had seemed so beautiful when she had first noticed it with Clark now seemed to be watching her every move.

Mrs. Gurney came back into the room, carrying a portable phone. Walking to the window, she stood directly next to the seagull. She turned to face Lily.

For a second, Lily's eyesight blurred. Mrs. Gurney's brown eyes reminded her of the seagull's red eye. She blinked. The fearsome image was gone. Mrs. Gurney took a step forward. She looked at Lily sympathetically and punched a number into the phone. Lily played with the lace on the front of her nightgown. Mrs. Gurney was going to give an excuse for how she couldn't reach Aunt Andrea. She had no intention of staying calm. She would get back to her aunt's apartment if she had to crawl there. "They're calling your aunt off the casino floor," said Mrs. Gurney.

Lily glared at her, glad to have caught Mrs. Gurney in an outright lie. "My aunt doesn't work on the casino floor. She works for the restaurant in the casino."

Mrs. Gurney shrugged her shoulders. Lily felt another shiver of glee. Mrs. Gurney was the one who hated people who shrugged. First she had caught her in a lie and then in a shrug. Mrs. Gurney wasn't perfect after all.

Lily picked up the teacup. She remembered spilling it, but she didn't remember filling it. Curlicues of smoke rose from the cup. How had the tea stayed so hot? The smell was enticing. She took a sip. Her throat was parched. The tea felt good and sweet going down.

"Oh, thank goodness, I got hold of you," said Mrs. Gurney in a loud voice. "Yes, Lily seems physically all right, but she's confused. She wants to talk to you."

Mrs. Gurney handed the phone to Lily.

"Aunt Andrea?" Lily's voice sounded tentative, as if she couldn't trust her own vocal cords.

"Lily," said Aunt Andrea. "Sweetie. Your voice sounds so weak. Are you feeling better?"

"Did you know I was here?" Lily asked.

"Of course," said Aunt Andrea. "I saw you yesterday. Right after the doctor. Don't you remember?"

Lily rubbed her eyes. She didn't want to admit that she has no memory of her aunt's visit—no memory of a doctor—nothing. "When am I coming home?" she asked. She could hear that she was almost whimpering.

"Home?" repeated Aunt Andrea, as if Lily were speaking a foreign language. "Your mother is still in New Mexico."

"I meant *your* home," Lily said softly into the telephone. She could hear the bells and noise of the casinos over the phone.

"Sweetie . . . I'll be over to see you as soon as I can."

"You don't have to come here. I can just take a taxi back to the apartment."

"You can't be in my apartment alone—put Mrs. Gurney back on." Aunt Andrea sounded impatient. Reluctantly, Lily handed the phone back to Mrs. Gurney. She turned her back on Lily and whispered into the phone.

Lily took another sip of the tea. Aunt Andrea had sounded almost annoyed at her. She felt so tired. Mrs. Gurney pushed the Off button on the phone. She frowned. "Your aunt will come as soon as she can." She tucked the covers in around Lily's legs.

"So the doctor was really here," Lily mumbled. She had begun to sweat again.

Mrs. Gurney nodded. "Yes, you spoke to the doctor. You even agreed to do as he said to try to get better."

Lily felt guilty. "What did I promise?"

"To drink fluids and to rest," said Mrs. Gurney. Her voice was gentle. She picked up the teapot. Steam still rose from the spout. She refilled Lily's cup and held it out to her. Lily swallowed. Her eyes felt heavy. She had lost three days out of her life. Her mother believed in out-of-body experiences. But this was more terrifying. Lily knew where her body had been—in bed in Mrs. Gurney's house—but where had the rest of her gone?

CLARK THOUGHT ABOUT THE MOMENT HIS SOUL HAD FELT AT REST, HOLDING LILY IN HIS ARMS IN THE ROOM FILLED WITH ROSES. He was scared for Lily. He had never been scared for anyone before. Was there a way for him to finally be at peace *and* to save Lily? He didn't know. The scent from those imaginary roses filled his nostrils. He ditched his rolling chair under the Boardwalk. He had no patience with tourists. He couldn't chitchat. He couldn't work and he didn't care. He paced the Boardwalk, walking back and forth past Mrs. Gurney's house. He stared up at the stained glass window, thinking about Lily, and about himself.

He had never spent a summer like this. Usually, the summers were the only time he was alive. It was his time to work his con games on the idiots, his time to flirt with girls usually too stupid to realize that he was just in it for the conquest.

Now he spent all his time worrying and longing for Lily, and she lay sick. He sneaked into the health club at Bally's and tried to exhaust himself. He climbed mountains on the StairMaster, bench pressed his weight. But nothing worked. He found no release.

When he was younger, his mother had taken him to

a succession of therapists, some recommended by the school, some she had found herself. The therapists all warned about Clark's lack of attachment. Clark could remember one therapist, one of the kindest, talking to him very earnestly about what he was missing. "A child who grows up without ties can become a man without bonds—someone who belongs to no one—it is a lonely life that you're sitting on, Clark."

Even as young as eleven, Clark thought of bonds as the iron chains that secured slaves. Slaves had bonds and ties. Besides, his mother had enough ties and bonds for both of them. Until he met Lily, he had managed to live a life without ties, a life of endless summers. Each summer was completely new. He was free to invent for himself whatever identity he chose. It would all disappear by September. Now he had actually met someone with whom he felt a tie—and the irony was that if he let himself feel love for Lily, he would destroy the very thing that kept him alive.

When it got dark, he left the casinos and walked down the Boardwalk. When he got to the Gurney mansion, he climbed up on the railing of the Boardwalk and watched the shadows fall on the bed on the lawn. The light from inside the rooms gave an added richness to the colors in the stained glass. He sat on the outside railing of the Boardwalk, leaning in and staring at the house. He would have to do something soon, something to bring things to a head.

A woman with an elaborate beehive hairdo passed by him. He recognized Lily's aunt from the night he had followed them on the Boardwalk. Lily had said that her aunt would like him. Lily actually believed that Clark could enter her circle and be warmed by it.

He watched as Lily's aunt turned into the walkway toward Mrs. Gurney's house. She rang the doorbell and was let inside. He licked his lips. He positioned himself outside on the lawn where he could at least look up and see the light on in the room that Lily was staying in.

Inside the room, Lily jerked to a sitting position. Everything was blurry. A light was on over the mirror, but the rest of the room was dark. She felt a cool hand on her cheek.

"Sweetie," said a voice.

"Mom," Lily murmured. The hand continued to stroke her cheek. She opened her eyes and saw her aunt. "I thought you were Mom."

Aunt Andrea took Lily's hand and started to stroke it, her thumb gently massaging Lily's palm. "Are you feeling better?" she asked.

Lily nodded. "I want to go home."

Lily watched her aunt's face. Andrea didn't look happy at the news. She wouldn't meet Lily's eyes. "Sweetie, guess what? My promotion came through. I can be a dealer. They've even put me in an accelerated class on dealing."

"That's great," said Lily. "You can teach me how to deal blackjack while I recover at your house."

"Well, you see," said Aunt Andrea, hesitating. "That's the problem. When I'm not working I'm in class. The doctor told me that he thinks you need somebody around all the time to help you eat and get back your strength."

"It's back," said Lily. She pulled down the covers.

"Lily, I don't think you should get out of bed," said Aunt Andrea.

Lily stood up. She wobbled to the window. She leaned against it, her shadow momentarily blocking out the light from the room. Clark saw her shadow outlined against the window. He wanted to reach out and touch it. He felt locked out, standing in the dark.

Lily was unaware of Clark's presence. Her over-whelming emotion was fatigue. Her muscles felt like water. Never, not even after playing an overtime soc-cer game in ninety-five degree heat and ninety-eight percent humidity, had she felt so weak. And she felt trapped. Aunt Andrea didn't want her, her mother was still frolicking out in the desert, and she was stuck. She almost couldn't bear to look at her aunt.

"What a lovely nightgown," said Aunt Andrea, as if searching for a neutral subject.

"I hate it," said Lily, looking down at the roses. "I think there's a T-shirt in one of the drawers, can you get it for me?"

"But this nightgown is so feminine and pretty. Where did you get it?"

"Mrs. Gurney gave it to me."

"You really do need to rest. Your face looks drawn, and your eyes don't have any sparkle."

"I'm tired," Lily finally admitted. She felt defeated.

She allowed her aunt to get her back into bed and to tuck the covers around her feet.

Mrs. Gurney appeared at the door. She was dressed in a red silk print dress. It fit her body perfectly. She was wearing black patent leather high heels. "Andrea," she said familiarly. "How do you think she's doing?"

"Oh, Mrs. Gurney, she just doesn't seem herself."

"You must call me Kitty," said Mrs. Gurney with a smile. "Remember, I asked you to call me Kitty once before." Mrs. Gurney made it sound as if she would prefer not to have to ask again.

"Kitty," said Andrea. She rolled the word around on her tongue, relishing the sound of it.

"I brought some tea and a little soup and toast for Lily."

"Oh, that's so kind of you," gushed Aunt Andrea. "I was just telling Lily about my promotion. I'm so thrilled. I know you said you had nothing to do with it, but that little word you put in for me, I know it made all the difference."

Mrs. Gurney smiled. Lily noticed that she had a tiny bit of lipstick on her teeth. "It gives me such pleasure to see a young woman like you getting ahead. When my husband died, we owned a few of the old hotels, and when the casinos came in, I tried to learn as much about the business as I could. Of course, I hoped that my son would be able to take over . . ." She paused. She looked straight at Lily. "But that was not to be." She poured a cup of tea and handed it to

Lily. She poured another cup for Aunt Andrea.

Aunt Andrea took the tea. "I know your son's death was tragic for you."

"You can't know," said Mrs. Gurney with a determined look on her face.

"I lost my brother, Lily's father, to a drowning accident."

Mrs. Gurney nodded at Lily knowingly, as if pleased that they shared a secret. The drownings bound them together. Lily kicked at the sheets that were pulled over her legs. "There, dear. You mustn't allow yourself to be agitated," warned Mrs. Gurney.

Lily waited. She was certain that Mrs. Gurney would probe at her father's death, ask questions, pry. But she surprised Lily. She let the subject drop.

"We just hate to be an imposition to you," said Aunt Andrea hesitantly.

"Taking care of Lily is something I want to do. I've told her that. Of course, if you feel uncomfortable about it . . ."

"Oh, no," said Aunt Andrea quickly. "With my new job, I am just so grateful." Aunt Andrea picked up the teacup from the bed table and held it to Lily's lips. Lily took a sip. Her aunt put her hand on her forehead. "She feels feverish. I wish I could get hold of her mother, but for the two weeks that she's on the vision quest there is no way to contact her—short of a dire emergency."

"Oh, the doctor assures us that it's nothing that serious," said Mrs. Gurney. "No need to get in touch with her mother. A 'vision quest'? What exactly is that?"

"I'm not sure. Lily's mother has always had a fondness for the occult. It's apparently some Native American ritual," said Aunt Andrea.

Mrs. Gurney smiled a noticeably disapproving smile. "Lily's mother has always taken good care of Lily," said Aunt Andrea quickly. "She holds down a good job as a school secretary."

"I'm sure she's a fine mother," said Mrs. Gurney. "You can tell that by the way Lily behaves—not like some of the kids that I've seen around. By the way, what do you know about her friend, Clark DeLuge?"

Lily choked on a little of the tea. Aunt Andrea looked very uncomfortable. "I don't know. Lily? Who is he?"

Lily was having trouble remembering anything. Had she really never told her aunt about Clark? She rubbed her eyes. "He's a friend," she managed to say. "I don't have many friends in Atlantic City."

Mrs. Gurney gave Lily a patronizing smile. "When you're feeling better, I'll introduce you to some nice people."

"Clark *is* nice," snapped Lily.

Mrs. Gurney didn't answer. She leaned over and fluffed Lily's pillow. Lily hated having her pillow fluffed. As soon as Mrs. Gurney finished, Lily deliberately punched and scrunched the pillow so that it was more to her liking. She fished under it to make sure Mrs. Gurney hadn't taken Clark's handkerchief. But it was there, and holding it felt reassuring.

Aunt Andrea stood up. She gave Lily a kiss. "I'll stop in and see you tomorrow."

"The doctor promised to stop in tomorrow also," said Mrs. Gurney.

"Kitty, you must be the only person who can get a doctor to make house calls these days," bubbled Aunt Andrea. Lily was disgusted with the way her aunt was fawning over Mrs. Gurney.

"Oh, he's an old friend," said Mrs. Gurney. "You know, the hospital is one of my main charities."

"Yes, of course. There's a wing named after you, isn't there?"

The two women left the room. Lily listened to their voices droning on and on in the hallway. The lace of her nightgown began to itch. Lily scratched her neck. It felt as if a thousand mosquitoes had found a home in the lace, attracted to the roses. The itching drove her crazy, but nothing she could do would relieve it.

CLARK ROLLED IN THE SAND. He slapped at a mosquito. His hair was full of sand. He needed a shower. He had been bitten by a horde of mosquitoes in the night. He scratched the side of his face so hard that he drew blood. He stood up, kicking his bedroll out of the way.

He licked the blood from his fingers, tasting its saltiness—the saltiness that reminded him that like everyone else, he came from the sea. He rubbed his face, feeling the stubble. He climbed up onto the Boardwalk. He passed Mrs. Gurney's house. The sweet smell of the roses made him want to vomit. He glanced up at the stained glass window. Poor Lily. She would never get out of there alive. Alive. What a word—a *life*. How many lives was one life worth?

He walked along the Boardwalk to the public baths where he showered. He could feel the red bumps from the mosquitoes. They seemed to have bitten him all over, as if the mosquitoes wanted to remind him that they could drink his blood at will. Was blood that attracted mosquitoes really worth the terrible cost? Clark knew he was being melodramatic, but he was not sure that his existence was worth anything to anybody. It was opposite—the longer he existed, the higher the cost.

Clark waited until the attendant was dealing with someone else, and then he stole a towel that would have cost a quarter. He walked to the mirror and looked at himself. He saw the scratches on his cheek. His eyes looked dead to him. The only animation in them came from rage. Was rage really a good excuse to go on? He didn't think so. He put his jeans back on. He stole some quarters out of the attendant's tip glass. It was time to stop playing with his rage. It was time to act. He left the public baths to find a telephone.

When Lily woke up, Mrs. Gurney was in the bedroom, sitting in a chair in the corner, with an easel facing the stained glass window. A crystal glass sat by her easel. Every time she picked up the glass, she shook the ice in it, making an irritating sound.

Everything irritated Lily. "This nightgown itches like crazy," she complained. She picked at the lace.

"You've probably sweated in that gown," said Mrs. Gurney. "There's a fresh nightgown at the end of your bed." Lily looked down at the end of the bed. The nightgown lying there was identical to the one she had on.

"Go change," said Mrs. Gurney. She smiled. She seemed in a good mood. "The doctor is coming to see you."

Lily climbed out of bed. She felt a little stronger. She didn't have to hold on to the walls. She wanted to make sure that she stayed awake for the doctor. She went into the bathroom. She had been too sick to really see it before. Like the rest of the guest room, it was swimming in roses. There were roses painted on the porcelain sink, and even the faucets were gold sculpted roses.

She stood close to the mirror. Her hair was sticking out in all directions. She didn't like seeing herself in the mirror. Deep shadows rimmed her eyes, like a raccoon. She forced herself not to look away from her image. She had seen eyes like hers once before. After her father died, her mother's eyes changed. She couldn't focus. Every time her mother had looked at her, Lily felt as if she were being looked through— not at. Grief had made her mother blind—not literally. The change in the way her mother looked at her had frightened Lily more than anything else during that horrible time.

Later, her mother would try to talk to Lily about grief—how despair was a stage that had to be lived through—but Lily hadn't wanted to listen. Lily stripped and stood in the shower. She held her face up and let the water splash over her face, neck and chest. She took a washcloth and scrubbed herself roughly. She washed her legs, surprised to see how strong they still looked. They gave her courage. She had always loved how far and fast her legs could carry her. She stepped out of the shower and looked at herself again in the mirror.

The shadows around her eyes had not gone away, but there was a flicker in her pupils, a flicker of fury.

She was angry at being sick. Sick and tired of illness. She opened the door to go back to the bedroom. She had almost walked out naked. She put on the night-gown and matching robe. She made a decision. Her anger was a secret. She would not reveal it to anyone. Her mother, whom everyone thought was so open, actually believed in secrets. "You are allowed your secrets, Lily," she told her. "You own them." They were strange words from a woman who didn't believe in ownership, who would never even say that they "owned" their cat. "Mom," whispered Lily to herself. "I miss you.

"May I open the window?" Lily asked when she came out of the bathroom.

"Oh, I wouldn't do that. You know, people can see right into this bedroom from the Boardwalk. That's why I had the stained glass put in. I didn't want my boy to have strangers looking in at him."

"This was your son's bedroom?" Lily couldn't imagine a boy subjected to this feminine and dainty bedroom. "Did he like this room?" Lily asked. She was curious. The boy was supposed to have been about her age when he died. She couldn't imagine any boy wanting to live in this room.

"Of course, it didn't look the way it does now," said Mrs. Gurney. "I think people who keep the room of a dead person as a shrine are being maudlin."

Lily gawked. This from a woman who put her dead son's bed out on the lawn! Mrs. Gurney sat back in

her chair as if she had just scored a point in a game
in which she knew all the rules, and Lily was an ama-
teur. "No, everything is different except the window.
I had the stained glass window made from a sketch
that my son did when he was just eleven. He was a
very talented artist. He loved the sea, much as your
father loved it."

"I never told you that my father loved the sea,"
said Lily.

"Oh," said Mrs. Gurney. "I thought you did.
Perhaps I imagined it, or your aunt told me. You
know, as we get older, we sometimes get confused."
Lily did not think that Mrs. Gurney was confused.

Lily decided to play Mrs. Gurney's game—change
the subject abruptly and see where the chips landed.
"I was worried that you'd be offended by my bringing
a tour to your house. You must hate people coming
to stare at the bedroom on the lawn."

"Well," said Mrs. Gurney. "If I really wanted to
keep my grief private, I wouldn't have put the bed out
there, would I?" She looked at Lily shrewdly.

"Did you want the bed to be a warning?" Lily asked
her. "I mean for people to realize that there is a dangerous undertow."

"It's not a warning," said Mrs. Gurney. "The bed
waits for my son to come back. That's why it stays
dry for him. When he first comes back, he's always
cold and wet. Then when he's warm, he's fine. He
loves the summertime."

Lily shuddered. "What do you mean 'when he first

comes back'? Have you ever seen him?"

Mrs. Gurney smiled and took a sip of her drink. "We're all allowed our fantasies, aren't we?"

"It must have been terrible, losing your son like that."

"You never get over it," said Mrs. Gurney simply.

Despite herself, Lily felt a wave of sympathy for Mrs. Gurney. Her mother always talked about the fact that Lily's father would always be with them. Her mother warned Lily that they could never pretend that he hadn't existed. He existed. He had loved, and now he was gone. There was no way to make that fact go away.

Mrs. Gurney was no different from anyone else who had to live with the fact that someone they loved had died. The bed sat out on the lawn because she was afraid to admit to herself that her son was dead. Lily's mother would have felt sorry for Mrs. Gurney and treated her kindly.

"Lily, dear," says Mrs. Gurney. "You seem a million miles away."

Lily swallowed. "I'm right here."

"You know the pain of losing someone you love. Sip some tea," said Mrs. Gurney softly. "I'll just sit here and make a sketch of you." She went back to her easel. The phone rang again. It was ringing in the room, but Lily knew distinctly that her room had no phone in it. Mrs. Gurney ignored it. She sat there placidly sketching with a charcoal pencil.

"The phone?" Lily said.

Mrs. Gurney shrugged. "I don't believe in being a slave to a ringing mechanism."

The ringing mechanism had a will of its own. The phone rang over a dozen times. Finally, Mrs Gurney pulled a cordless phone off the easel rest. She clicked the receiver open. "Yes," she snapped.

She listened for several seconds. She clicked the phone closed. "I find those solicitation phone calls so annoying," she said to Lily. "They call at all hours."

"Yeah, my mom hates them too," Lily said. "Although Mom always feels sorry for the person who's been hired to make the calls. She talks to them and then she winds up either buying something we don't need or giving some money to a charity. But that's my mom."

"You have to be very selective when you give to charity," said Mrs. Gurney. "Otherwise, you're just scattering your money around." Lily decided that she liked the way that her mom was spontaneously generous.

The phone rang again. Mrs. Gurney snapped open her phone. "I told you, she cannot be disturbed. This is a terrible time to be calling." She hung up.

Lily frowned. "Who can't be disturbed? Was it Clark?"

Mrs. Gurney deliberately looked at her sketch.

"If it was Clark, I want to talk to him," said Lily defiantly. "He's my friend."

Mrs. Gurney laughed. "Lily, I have better things to do with my time than to interfere with a teenager's love life. I was only thinking of your health. If you think it is important to talk to him, by all means do so."

Mrs. Gurney pulled a piece of paper out of her pocket. It had a phone number written on it. "Is this where he lives?" Lily asked eagerly. She realized that Clark had never given her his phone number.

"I don't know where he lives," said Mrs. Gurney. "This is the number he gave me if he needed to be reached." She had a funny smile on her face, as if enjoying a private joke. She handed the phone to Lily.

Lily punched in the number. "Men's room," said a voice.

Lily hung up. She looked accusingly at Mrs. Gurney. "That was a cruel joke," she said.

"What was cruel?"

"You gave me the number of a men's room," said Lily.

"It was the number he gave me," said Mrs. Gurney. "If someone was making a cruel joke, it wasn't me."

Lily stared at the phone. Why would Clark have given her the number of a men's room? It was like a fifth grade bad joke. Perhaps she had dialed wrong.

She punched in the number again. The same voice answered,"Men's room."

"Is a Clark DeLuge there?" asked Lily in a soft voice.

"Yo, anybody named Clark here? Some chick wants her superman."

Lily heard some men laughing. She almost hung up, but a second later, she heard Clark's voice.

"Listen, if I'm a son of a bitch, what does that make you," he said, his voice menacing. "I want—"

"Clark," Lily interrupted.

"Lily?" Clark's voice changed completely. He laughed. "I thought you were somebody else."

Lily wondered who he thought she was. She had never heard that tone of voice from him. "Did you call me? Mrs. Gurney gave me this number."

Clark scratched one of his mosquito bites. Now that he had Lily on the phone, he felt tongue-tied. What could he really tell her? The truth. She wouldn't believe it, and would the truth save her? He doubted it. The only sure way to save her from himself was to end it all. But would he really have the courage? He didn't know.

Clark rubbed his face. The mosquito bites mocked him. Even the mosquitoes knew that he wouldn't give up his warm blood willingly. How his mother would laugh at the idea of Clark in love! "Love means sacrifice," his mother used to tell him, although her idea of sacrifice was vodka without ice.

"Lily, is she in the room with you?" Clark said.

Lily glanced at Mrs. Gurney. She had no doubt whom Clark meant. She nodded, and then realized that Clark couldn't see her nod.

"Yes," she said haltingly.

Clark laughed. "Perfect," he said.

Lily couldn't quite understand his mood. He acted as if he wanted to talk to her, but first there was the long silence and then just a stupid laugh. He hadn't even asked how she was feeling.

"How have you been?" she asked.

Clark shrugged. "Not good," he said.

"Are you sick too?" Lily sounded alarmed.

Clark shook his head. He held the phone away from his face. Lily wanted to know if he was sick. What a joke! Sick! He was sick and tired of every aspect of his existence.

"Are you?" Lily insisted.

"No," Clark said into the receiver.

He still didn't ask her how she was. He was making Lily angry. "Why did you call?" Lily asked.

Clark sighed. What could he tell her?

"Just to chat," he finally said. A man, pinkly sunburned, wearing a pair of wide-legged shorts in splashy fabric of Day-Glo pinks and greens stretched over his belly, wanted to use the phone. Clark motioned him to go away.

Lily scowled into the phone. "To chat!" she repeated. "You haven't seen me since that day I was so sick—and all you want to do is chat!"

"No . . . that's not what I meant," Clark said quickly, realizing that the phone conversation was going from bad to worse. The man in the shorts scowled at Clark impatiently.

"Well what?" demanded Lily.

"I just . . . "

"Just what?"

"I don't know," said Clark angrily. "I guess I miss you. Look. I should go. Somebody needs to use the phone."

"You guess you miss me," repeated Lily. It was so little. She hung up.

Lily lay against the pillows and stared at the stained glass window. He guessed he missed her. She sobbed so hard that her chest hurt. She rolled over, burying her head in the pillows so that Mrs. Gurney wouldn't hear her sobs. Her mother was gone. Her aunt was working too hard to be there for her—and Clark! He *guessed* he missed her. He hadn't even asked her how she was feeling. Who knew what kind of game or scam he was playing? He was simply another in the long line of bad choices. She balled up his handkerchief and threw it across the room.

LILY HEARD THE DOORBELL RING. A few moments later, Mrs. Gurney entered the room with a man who looked about sixty years old. He was mostly bald, dressed in a plaid shirt and gray pants. "How are you feeling?" the man asked.

"Who are you?" Lily asked. She quickly wiped her eyes. She didn't want Mrs. Gurney to know that she had been crying.

"I'm Dr. Kemika," he said. He smiled at her, and took off his half glasses. "We met before."

"I don't remember," Lily admitted.

"That's all right," he said kindly. "I'm glad to see you seem to be getting a little stronger. I've done all the blood tests. Your white count is fine. But if you're not having an infection, and it's not the flu, I'm puzzled. And the short-term memory loss is worrisome. It most often happens with a concussion, but Mrs. Gurney and your aunt tell me that you haven't fallen."

Suddenly Lily remembered the feel of Jimmy's head as it had jerked into her chin when she and Clark were rescuing him. She could feel her neck snap back as sharply as she had felt Clark's anger on the phone. She wondered where Clark had gone when he had hung up. She didn't even know if she would ever see him again.

"Could you get a concussion if you're hit on the chin?" Lily asked the doctor.

Mrs. Gurney was staring at her. "You mean, punched?" asked Dr. Kemika.

"No," said Lily. "But the other day, in the water, I kind of hit my chin."

The doctor reached down and took Lily's face in his hands. His hands were soft. He felt along her cheekbones. "There is a slight swelling on the right side. And a concussion doesn't have to come from a blow to the head. It can happen if you suddenly jerk the spinal cord."

Lily felt a wave of relief. She had a concussion once on the soccer field. It was scary, but the symptoms went away. It was true that she had never had a concussion that had left her as weak as this. But still it was a rational explanation. "I've had a concussion before. I once collided with this girl on the soccer field. She was built like a Mack truck. But I didn't feel this sick. Why would this concussion make me sweat like this? Is that normal?"

The doctor looked at Mrs. Gurney over Lily's head. "Let me worry about the diagnosis. Your job is just to get well."

Lily didn't like the way doctor was treating her, as if her questions were "cute," and that she was too young to know exactly what was wrong with her.

The doorbell rang again. Mrs. Gurney went to get

it, leaving Lily alone with the doctor. "You are so lucky to have Mrs. Gurney taking care of you. She is a wonderful woman. I've always loved that stained glass window. When I was a young man, I used to walk by it every day. It's quite an honor to be allowed to stay in this room." The doctor poured himself a cup of tea, and then he refilled Lily's teacup. She took it automatically.

Aunt Andrea burst into the bedroom, followed by Mrs. Gurney. She gave Lily a big hug and kiss. Lily let her head rest on Aunt Andrea's shoulder. She felt safe in the arms of her aunt. Soon she'd be back in Aunt Andrea's apartment and out of this bedroom. Aunt Andrea rubbed Lily's back in small, comforting circles.

"We might have gotten to the bottom of Lily's mysterious illness," said the doctor. "Apparently, she was swimming and somehow got a concussion."

Aunt Andrea stopped rubbing Lily's back. She held Lily at arm's distance so that she could look into her face. "Swimming?" she demanded.

"Why is that such a shock?" asked Mrs. Gurney.

"Lily's always been afraid of the water," said Aunt Andrea. "She can't swim."

"Oh," said Mrs. Gurney.

"The important thing is that now that we know I just have a little concussion. I can go back to your apartment," said Lily eagerly. "Right, doctor?"

Aunt Andrea frowned. "Oh, dear," she said. "The casino signed me up for a special course on roulette. It's in Philadelphia, and I have to go for two nights. I didn't realize that Lily was well enough to come home so soon. I told them I could go."

"Of course you should go," said Mrs. Gurney. "Lily wouldn't want to stand in the way of your career, would you, Lily?"

Lily's hands were balled into fists. She felt like hitting somebody—smashing her fist into flesh and bone. Mrs. Gurney put her hand over Lily's fist. "There, there. I can see that you're upset. But you mustn't worry. I'm happy to take care of you."

The doctor ignored Lily's agitation. It was as if she didn't exist. He turned to Mrs. Gurney and chatted about some upcoming benefit for his hospital.

"Lily, I almost forgot," said Aunt Andrea. "You got a postcard from your mom. I brought it in my purse."

Aunt Andrea handed Lily the card. It showed a woman on a donkey in the canyon lands. There was both a rainbow and lightning in the sky over the canyon. Lily turned the postcard over. The artist, Diana Breyer, had called the drawing "Vision Quest." Lily glared at the card. The colors were too bright.

Lightning and thunder herald visions. Learn from the storms of your life! Be careful of those who want to drag you away from your true spirit. Her mother signed it with a heart.

Lily bit her lip. She imagined her mother in the desert finding her soul and she was furious. She ripped the card into pieces and flung them over the side of the bed. Her mother was questing for a vision. Suddenly Lily screamed. "You want a vision, Mom! How about this for a vision! Your only daughter is sweating every night in a strange bed! You'd rather be staring up at the moon. Well, your daughter is here on earth, Mom, and she's stuck in a dead boy's bedroom! *The dead boy's* mother, not you, tucks me into bed each night!"

"Lily, are you all right?" asked Aunt Andrea. She patted Lily on the back. "Doctor, are these coughing spells something to worry about?"

Lily choked. "Coughing spells?" she said.

"Yes, dear, just then. You were coughing as if you couldn't stop." With a shock Lily realized that she had only thought she was shouting out loud. Nobody had heard her. They thought she was coughing.

Lily looked down at her hands. She opened her fists. Her fingernails had dug into her palms, making deep half-moons into her flesh. She twisted her head toward the window and the seagull. The sweats had started again. She was soaked to the skin, as if she had been swimming.

19

CLARK'S KNUCKLES WERE RAW AND BLEEDING. He knelt at the water's edge, washing his hand in the salt water, squinting out at the sea. The poor slob in the shorts hadn't deserved a broken nose. "Totally unprovoked," he was sure the guy was telling the police.

Clark ran into the ocean. The police might look for him, but they wouldn't find him. Besides, one punch in the nose to a tourist didn't exactly make him a candidate for *America's Most Wanted.*

He swam out beyond the breakers. He felt the current pulling. He rolled over on his back and floated. He could just let it take him. Through the slits in his eyes, he looked up at the sun. The salt water in his eyes made rings around the sunlight. He swallowed some water and started to gag. Then he rolled over. With powerful strokes he swam farther out. Maybe he wouldn't come back.

Clark swam too far out. He knew it. He could feel the current dragging him at an angle away from the shore. He was tired of swimming now. His powerful arms felt like they had weights on them. He could barely break the surface. A wave lifted him. He had known people who had committed suicide this way. It was a strange death for a good swimmer. It appealed to him. You used your own strength to take you so far out that you could not return.

Once Clark had shrieked at his mother, "You'd be better off if I were dead." He stopped swimming for a moment and rubbed his eyes. How many years had it been? He could hardly remember. Why hadn't he shouted the truth? "I would be better off if *you* were dead."

He thought he could hear Lily's voice screaming out to him. He rode the top of a wave like a cork, lighter than any boat, lighter than any person. The water was his savior. He knew that. If he could ride the waves, they would take him—deep in his soul, he knew that he could trust the sea. But if he let them take him now, he couldn't help Lily, and next summer it would start all over again.

Lily drifted awake. She had been dreaming that she was playing soccer. She kicked the ball straight into the net. The boy playing center grabbed her in his arms, twirling her around, thumping her back in joy! It was Clark, a look of sheer pleasure on his face—the incredible joy that only teammates could share. Then suddenly they were off the field, away from the rest of the teams, Clark's arms still around her. His long hair was tangled and wet. She had felt wrapped in that hair—protected. The dream had been sensual, the hair caressing. She hadn't wanted to wake up.

Clark headed for the shore, forcing himself to kick.

Lily would die if he stayed out at sea. He couldn't leave without trying to save her. But he knew it would be a battle. He would have to go on the attack. He would have to be willing to risk everything.

His first battles had been with his mother, and he had always lost. His mother enjoyed teaching him to play chess because even when she was drunk, she could always beat him. Clark would sit at the chess set, his knuckles white as he held the intricately carved black horse tightly in his hand.

He loved his Black Knight. He tried to choose a square to put it somewhere where it would be safe, where she would not pounce. His mother would laugh at him. "You must never become too attached to one piece. That's a fatal error for a player," she instructed him. For all the times that he had laughed at, and even despised his mother, he knew she was right about that one lesson.

Clark dreaded their chess games, and yet he never refused to play. Even though Clark knew his mother would win, he took a perverse pleasure in trying to hold off her victory as long as possible. When he lost he never cried. After the game, when his king was toppled and the pieces were strewn around the board, his mother would make him set them up again for the next time. The chess pieces would just wait there for his next defeat. He never saw his mother play chess with anyone else. It was time for one last game, but this time Clark would choose the game, and it would not be chess.

He made it to the beach, exhausted. He rolled over on his back, feeling weak. He stood up, his legs trembling. He walked up the sand to where he had hidden his bedroll and knapsack. He pulled on a dry black T-shirt. Clark climbed up the stairs of the Boardwalk, ignoring the tourists and the other chair pushers. He walked to the soup kitchen run by the Catholic church directly behind the Riverboat Casino. He could have snuck into any of the casinos for the buffet, but somehow the soup kitchen appealed to him. He was much hungrier for human compassion than for food.

It was time for the warrior's last meal before the assault. He stood in line with the others, taking his plate of spaghetti. He asked for tea instead of coffee, and the volunteer replied "Certainly dear," perkily and quickly, as if she *loved* serving him. He gave her a tight smile, and she grinned back. "It's hot, be careful sipping it," she warned. "You don't want to burn yourself." Then she looked up and saw his eyes. Clark could see her recoil. She could see his rage and his despair, and she was smart enough to realize he was beyond her help. Burning his lips with hot tea was the least of his problems.

He ate his spaghetti quickly. He returned the plate and asked for another cup of tea. "Hot!" he requested.

She poured it for him without meeting his eyes. He took the paper cup and walked out of the church and past the casinos. He finished his tea and went back up under the Boardwalk where he stored his few belongings. He took his bedroll and tossed it at a guy in his sixties who had been sleeping under the Boardwalk for a week. The man had come to Atlantic City absolutely sure that he had a system for beating the odds at blackjack.

"Here. Take it. I won't need it anymore," said Clark. The man looked at him suspiciously. There was very little generosity under the Boardwalk.

"Where are you going?" he asked.

"I'm the Black Knight," said Clark sarcastically.

"If you're the Black Knight, where's your black horse?"

Clark thumped his chest melodramatically. "I'm a Black Knight in here. Where it counts."

The guy backed off, probably figuring that Clark was on something. He wasn't. Unless it was adrenaline. "I've got to do what Black Knights are born to do," he told the guy.

"What's that?"

"Slay the dragon," said Clark. Then he took off down the Boardwalk toward the bed.

20

"SIP SOME TEA, DEAR," SAID MRS. GURNEY. "Be careful, it's hot, don't burn your lips."

Lily stared down at the teacup. There were bits of leaves floating in her tea, like little pieces of bark. They circled round and round. Lily's hand was shaking. She put down the teacup. Mrs. Gurney got up from her seat. "Darling, are you all right? Here, let me help you."

Lily shook her head. She didn't want any tea, and she didn't want Mrs. Gurney calling her "dear" and "darling." Mrs. Gurney settled down in a chair next to the stained glass window.

Lily lay back on the bed, hearing the sound of Mrs. Gurney's paintbrush as it scratched against the canvas. Each brush stroke sounded exaggerated, as if it were wired for sound. The sound of the ice cracking in Mrs. Gurney's glass sounded like the snap of an avalanche. Lily's senses were extrasensitive. She tried to deepen her breathing.

After a while Mrs. Gurney left the room. Before leaving she covered her painting with a black cloth. Lily looked around, glad to be alone. She got out of bed. The seagull in the stained glass window looked as if it was shrieking at her. Its hooked beak was open.

Lily couldn't remember if it had always been open. She needed air.

She went to the window and tugged at the sash. The window wouldn't budge. Lily thought she could remember opening it before. But maybe that was simply another thing she was confused about. She tugged at the sash again. Her biceps quivered. She couldn't believe that she could have gotten weak so quickly.

Then she looked at the window closely. It had been nailed shut. She looked around the room, ready to smash the window through the pretty little seagull. She glanced at the easel. Lying next to the easel was a putty knife. Lily grabbed it. Her sleeve caught the cloth covering the portrait. The cloth dropped away. The thick paint on the portrait was still sticky to the touch.

Lily's dilated pupils stared back at her from the painting. Thick black waves of paint lapped at her hair. Although the eyes were painted in oil, Lily's other features had been outlined in pencil, but not yet painted in. She was dressed in the nightgown with pink roses. The whole painting seemed to be drowning in darkness and iridescent deep blue purples and yellows.

Lily's stomach heaved. She sank down on the floor, scared that she was going to vomit. The cloth from the easel lay by her feet, like the dense purple paint on the portrait. She pulled herself up, using the wall for support. She reached down for the cloth and covered up the easel. She could only breathe shallowly. She tried to still the terror, not quite understanding where it came from. She saw a glass of water on the easel rest. Her throat felt parched. She picked up the glass and sipped. She spit it back out, the alcohol in the drink burning her throat.

Perhaps the alcohol explained Mrs. Gurney's strange delusion that her son returned to the bed "cold and wet" every summer. Lily closed her eyes for a second. Mrs. Gurney drank. Sonny had told her that, but she had completely forgotten. It made everything seem simple, less sinister and more just plain sad. Lily put the glass back on the stand.

She did not want to be stuck one more moment in a house with a sad, drunk old woman. She used the putty knife to pry back the nails. The nails twisted but wouldn't move. Her nightgown ripped on one of the nails, scratching her arm. She touched the scratch, wiping away the little drops of red blood. She took hold of the putty knife and pried at the nail again. Finally one of the nails curled away from the window. She jimmied the other one loose.

The window slipped up easily. Fresh air blew in from the ocean, almost startling her—it felt as if the air belonged to another world—one that she had almost forgotten. It was almost dusk. She looked out at the sea. Then she glanced down at the dead boy's bed. The sheets were as tight and snug as always.

She breathed in and out. She began to feel better. She walked around the room, coming to the teacup. She picked it up and carried it to the window. Staring

down at the bed, she started to take a sip. She hesitated. Then without really knowing why, she poured
the contents out the window, watching it splash on
the rosebushes below.

She saw a shadow next to the bed on the lawn. The
figure moved out of the shadow of the tree. She
ducked down under the sill, not wanting to be seen.
Then the figure stepped closer. Clark was standing by
the bed, almost like a silent sentinel. He was wearing
a black shirt, and only his face glowed in the light as
the floodlights came on in the dusk.

21

CLARK SAW LILY LOOK DOWN AT HIM FROM THE WINDOW.
He felt relieved when he saw her throw out the contents
of her teacup. His power was working. She could receive
his warnings. He could enter her mind. He walked around
the bed, touching the blanket. He felt hyped up.

Inside the house, Lily heard footsteps on the
stairs. She didn't want Mrs. Gurney to see Clark.
Bolting for the bed, she lay down. She fluttered her
eyes, feeling like a bad actress. "I brought you some
fruit and some more tea," said Mrs. Gurney cheerily.
"You need to build up your stamina."

Mrs. Gurney sat by the painting. She picked up her
glass and sniffed it, without sipping it. It was almost
as if she could smell Lily's scent on the glass. She
lifted the cloth off the easel and frowned. Lily saw her
glance at the window. She felt the need to distract her.
"You know, I'm really curious about that painting.
When are you going to show it to me?"

"Soon enough," said Mrs. Gurney. They both
heard the wind blow against the open window. "I hope
we're not getting a hurricane," said Mrs. Gurney. "It's
early for the hurricane season, but they can strike
unexpectedly." She walked over to the window. Lily
was terrified Mrs. Gurney would discover Clark out

on her lawn. "Won't you tell me a little more about your son?" Lily asked.

Mrs. Gurney turned and smiled at her indulgently. "Why are you so interested in him all of a sudden?"

"I don't know. I'm living in his room. It's natural to be curious about him."

"Well, he was very caring, considerate and obedient."

Lily thought that made him sound like a well-trained puppy. "A regular Boy Scout."

"No, he never joined the Boy Scouts. When I was young, I couldn't wait to join the Girl Scouts. I suppose some people would say that my charitable activities are proof that I'm still a Girl Scout." She giggled girlishly. "I'll tell you a secret. When I went to Girl Scout camp, I got kicked out for drinking. We really knew how to have a good time."

Lily had seen other adults try to bond by telling risqué stories about their youth. Usually the stories were lame. "I bet you had some wonderful parties in this house."

"Oh yes," said Mrs. Gurney. "I've always thought fun was important. So many people don't, you know. It was a lesson I tried to teach my son—that life must be lived to the fullest. People today are such Puritans. But that always happens at a turn of the century. A millennium seems to bring out panic. People get fearful. I've never been afraid. Fear is for fools."

Lily wondered whether Mrs. Gurney was totally sane, never mind the vodka. Her son had drowned. Fear came with love, because if you loved someone they could die. Mrs. Gurney had to be lying about never being afraid.

Lily made an exaggerated farce out of yawning. She wanted Mrs. Gurney to think she was asleep. She tried to keep her face calm though she knew that if Mrs. Gurney looked closely, she'd see that she was faking. Sleeping faces aren't really calm—they twitch and are alive. Only people trying to fake sleep don't move.

After a few minutes, Mrs. Gurney leaned over the bed. "Rest, dear," she whispered. Lily smelled the rose oil perfume, but it didn't mask the alcohol on her breath. Mrs. Gurney kissed her on the cheek.

Clark walked up the path to the front door. Ringing the doorbell of the "drowned boy's" house was a badge of honor for some kids in Atlantic City, a rite of passage. Ring it and run away. Clark was not here to run away.

Something shrieked. The shriek came from a live seagull, crying out somewhere near. Lily heard the doorbell ring. She knew that it was Clark at the door. She went to the door of the bedroom, almost afraid to touch the knob, like a prisoner who comes to feel safe only inside her cell. For several minutes, she stood in front of the door, paralyzed. Then, she took hold of the doorknob and turned it. It rotated in her hand easily. She had never been locked in. She could have left any time she wanted. She started down the stairs toward Clark.

22

CLARK SAT ON ONE OF THE COUCHES IN THE LIVING ROOM. He saw Lily coming down the stairs, gripping the banister. He smiled at her. His smile betrayed nothing of what he was feeling.

He stood up, as if he were only being polite.

Mrs. Gurney frowned. "Lily, dear. If you had wanted to come down and visit, you should have put on a robe. I'll go get you one." She swept past Lily and went upstairs.

Lily was confused. Everything seemed so normal between Mrs. Gurney and Clark. Not as if Mrs. Gurney despised Clark. She lurched and grabbed on to the wall.

Clark handed her a bunch of flowers. "I brought these for you." Lily would not have been more surprised if he had handed her a bomb. He acted as if he was just making an obligatory sick call.

"Lilies of the valley," said Clark. Lily lowered her nose into the flowers and drank in the sweetness. Mrs. Gurney bustled back into the room, carrying a robe made out of matching material to the nightgown. Roses crept up the sleeves of the robe. She tugged at Lily's arms until she got her into the robe. Clark settled back on the couch.

"I didn't realize you were awake," said Mrs. Gurney. "When I looked in on you a while ago, you were sound asleep." She turned to Clark. "Lily hasn't been well enough to come downstairs before."

Clark picked up his teacup. He held his little finger out daintily. Wiping his fingers across his lips, he addressed Mrs. Gurney. "Kitty, you were going to show me your latest paintings."

"Kitty?" repeated Lily, not even aware she had said the word out loud. She was so shocked. When had Clark begun calling Mrs. Gurney Kitty?

Mrs. Gurney laughed flirtatiously. "I decided, Lily, that any friend of yours was a friend of mine. After all, now that Clark and I have had a little talk, I realized that I *have* known his family for a long time."

"Atlantic City is such a small town," said Clark in a bored voice. Lily wondered what kind of game he was playing. He had been into game playing from the day she met him.

Lily glanced around the living room. This was the first time she had been able to get a good look at Mrs. Gurney's other paintings. Interspersed among the beautiful Impressionist paintings were many portraits of teenage boys and girls—and each of them had a dark background of the sea. Each portrait was somehow similar to the one upstairs of her.

"Do you like the paintings?" Clark asked.

"No!" Lily shouted out the word. Mrs. Gurney sat on the couch sipping her tea. Was she pretending not to hear her or had the shout only been inside her head? The bed was cursed. Didn't the young fortune-teller warn her that something or someone was dragging her down? Hadn't her mother warned her against those who would drag her spirit away? Lily had dismissed the fortune-teller's words, thinking that at the most she had picked up on Reggie. She had been so angry at her mother that she had ripped up her card. But what if they both were right? What if Mrs. Gurney was dragging her down into depths from which she would never emerge?

Clark went to the table next to the couch and picked up his teacup. He sat down next to Mrs. Gurney. Lily could not let him drink it! The warning instinct that had caused her to pour out the tea before was ringing in her ears. Something in the woodsy flavor of the tea was poisoning her, dragging her down. Putting her own cup down, Lily pretended to totter. She knocked over the tea service and fell into Clark's lap, forcing the teacup out of his hand. The teacup dropped to the floor and broke.

Mrs. Gurney's and Clark's eyes locked on to each other.

"I'm sorry," said Lily. She hated the sound of her voice. She sounded like a little kitten mewling.

"It was an accident," said Clark.

"Obviously," said Mrs. Gurney. "It's not our first." Her voice was amused as if at some private joke. "Perhaps, Lily, you're not as well as you thought. Maybe you should go back to bed." She got off the couch and picked up the broken teacup pieces. "I'll get you a fresh cup," she said to Clark. She went to the sideboard near the chess set.

"Do you play?" she asked Clark.

"I haven't in a long time," answered Clark.

"It's such a fascinating game," said Mrs. Gurney. "One always feels either that you're going to crush your opponent or be crushed."

"Better to crush," said Clark.

Lily stayed where she had fallen on Clark's lap. She wasn't sure what she was going to do, but she knew she was not going to move. She shivered.

"You're clammy," Clark said.

"It's her illness," said Mrs. Gurney with a slightly martyred sigh. She handed a fresh cup to Clark.

Lily glared at her. With Lily still in his lap, Clark lifted the cup to his lip. "Don't drink the tea," Lily whispered urgently into his ear, pretending that she couldn't keep her head up and leaning her head against his chest. Clark put down the teacup and draped his jacket around her shoulders. He gave no indication that he had heard her. He put his hand on her forehead. "She's sweating. She's soaking."

"I knew she shouldn't be out of bed," said Mrs. Gurney.

"I'll take her upstairs," said Clark.

"I'll help you," said Mrs. Gurney. She got up and took Lily's arm. Lily gave a violent shiver. "You're chilled, dear. You'll be better off in bed." Mrs. Gurney's hand felt like a vise on her arm. They half carried her up the stairs. "Whatever it is, her illness has left her so moody," said Mrs. Gurney. "Sometimes she seems like she's ready to jump out of her skin."

Lily shuddered. She saw herself jumping out of her skin. She would be nothing but muscles and bone—raw flesh. She thought about the way her fingers puckered like prunes when she was in the bath. As a person drowned, did they want to jump out of their skin? Had that happened to her father?

She cried out, "I won't jump out of my skin."

"Lily," said Clark tenderly. "It's all right."

"Nothing is all right," insisted Lily. She couldn't even trust her voice. What had Clark heard? Had he even heard her words?

At the top of the stairs, Mrs. Gurney let go of Lily's arm. "Clark, maybe you can talk some sense into her," she said to Clark. "If she would just rest, she'd get better and could go home." Mrs. Gurney made it sound as if she couldn't wait to get rid of Lily. Clark steered Lily back into the bedroom and sat her on the edge of the bed. He closed the door tight.

Lily pushed at his chest angrily. "Why did you bring me up here? I wanted to get out! I can't stay here," she hissed at him. "I can't. I can't. I *am* jumping out of my skin. And if I do, I'll die."

Lily waited for Clark to tell her she was crazy, or worse, that her words made no sense. "It's okay, Lily. I understand."

Lily took a deep breath. He didn't think she was crazy.

Clark could see Lily jumping out of her skin. She

was that desperate to escape. And he wanted to help her. He had come to the house to save her—to get her out. But it was too soon. He needed more time. Coming to this house made him realize he still wasn't ready. Was it indulgent to ask for one last night. Yes, but it would be his last. There would be no more games, no more teasing. No more lies. Belonging to someone was not evil. Lily could belong to him the way no other girl ever had and he would set her free.

He put his arms around her, pinning her arms at her side. He drew her back down on the bed. "I hate this room," she said, looking around. "Those roses drive me crazy. Clark, I think there's something in the tea." She waited for Clark to tell her that she was being melodramatic and stupid.

Clark didn't look at her as if she were demented. He picked up her hand. "Go on," he said. She looked straight into his eyes. His eyes looked more brown than green today. The night had turned them dark.

"My aunt has gone off to Philadelphia. I suspect that somehow Mrs. Gurney arranged that. I think I'm going to end up dead or drowned. I want out of here tonight."

"I need just a little bit of time," begged Clark. "Pretend to get along with Mrs. Gurney. Tomorrow night, in the middle of the night, find a way to get out of the house. Once you're out, I can help you. Meet me out by the bed on the lawn tomorrow at midnight."

"All I've been doing is pretending. I can't stand it another night."

"She'll be back any minute," warned Clark. "It's just one night. I'll give up everything for you."

Lily heard his words. There was a knock at the door.

"Clark, is everything all right in there?" asked Mrs. Gurney.

"Yes, ma'am," said Clark. He went to the door and opened it for Mrs. Gurney. Lily wished he would have barred it shut. Locked it tight.

"Lily, are you feeling better?" asked Mrs. Gurney. Her voice was perfectly normal.

"I was just leaving," said Clark. "I'll come see Lily again."

"Yes, I think Lily would like that," said Mrs. Gurney. She closed the door to the bedroom.

Lily crawled under the covers. She tried to tell herself that she could stand anything for one day—even Mrs. Gurney. Clark hadn't thought she was insane. Clark loved her. Her mother had always promised her that love didn't and couldn't make sense. Her mother had fallen in love with her father in an instant. Tomorrow, she and Clark would be out in the fresh air again. They would be back with people, walking on the Boardwalk, hand in hand.

23

CLARK FELT GUILTY. He was betraying Lily by asking for one more night, but he wasn't quite ready. If Lily learned what he had told Mrs. Gurney she would hate him for it. But he needed one more night, and he had to be sure that Lily didn't try to take off on her own.

All night he walked the Boardwalk, savoring the atmosphere, wondering what it would be like to finally let go. For the last time he wandered in and out of the casinos, enjoying the insistent *ding ding ding* of the slot machines when they gave out a big win. He listened to the familiar *chink chink chink* of quarters and silver dollars falling into the troughs. He knew that the casinos timed the winners. The slots went off every ninety seconds. When anybody walked into a casino, they'd always felt the next time they'd be the lucky one. Even losers felt they still had a chance.

Clark enjoyed the sound and light show of the slot machines and the video poker games. The casinos were all designed so that once you entered you always forgot where the exit was. They were like a maze, and Clark could have gotten a Scout merit badge for finding his way through them. He watched the people, ever hopeful. His time for hope was long past. He knew that he'd never be one of them. He never was. If he was going to help Lily, he'd have to give up hope.

He stuck a quarter in the video poker game. He had always loved poker. He waited for the royal flush. It would be fitting. But he didn't get it. Instead he got a straight. He left twenty dollars of credit in the machine. Some lucky player would come along and not believe his or her luck. A lucky chance was his legacy.

He walked outside of the casino. The first rays of light hit the ocean. His ocean. His home. He walked down to the beach and turned away from the casinos back to Mrs. Gurney's house. He was ready for the endgame.

24

CLARK HAD ASKED LILY TO WAIT, AND SHE WOULD, BUT THAT DIDN'T MEAN THAT SHE HAD TO STAY IN HER ROOM. She remembered feeling foolish the night before when she had worried that the door was locked.

She got out of bed, determined to explore the house on her own. The doorknob wouldn't turn in her hand. She tried putting her weight behind it. Perhaps the moisture from the ocean had swelled the wood. But the door wouldn't move. Mrs. Gurney had locked her in! Somehow Mrs. Gurney knew of Clark's plan and she was determined to keep her here—locked in forever.

Lily banged hard on the door. She kept it up until her fists were raw and red. She would not let Mrs. Gurney bury her in this bedroom. Suddenly, Lily watched as the doorknob turned. "What is this shouting about?" demanded Mrs. Gurney. She entered the room carrying a teapot.

Furiously, Lily swept her arm out and the teapot fell to the floor. It smashed. Mrs. Gurney jumped in her high heels, narrowly missing the splashing hot water.

"What was the racket about?" asked Mrs. Gurney.

"Why was I locked in?" Lily demanded.

Mrs. Gurney bent down to pick up the pieces of

broken china. "I locked you in for your safety," she said calmly.

"Inside the house?" Lily said sarcastically.

"I didn't want to, but your friend suggested it."

"What do you mean?"

"Your friend, Clark. I thought it was cute the way he brought you flowers. He suggested that for your own safety I lock you in for the night so that you didn't go wandering around the house and hurt yourself. I assure you—I would never have done it on my own."

"You're lying. Clark wouldn't have told you that. I want to leave this house."

Mrs. Gurney stood up with the pieces of broken crockery in her hand. She opened her hand and discarded the broken pieces into the wastepaper basket. They made a clanging noise. "Then go," she said softly. "I have certainly lost enough china. You are not a prisoner here."

"Right, just leave," said Lily mockingly.

Mrs. Gurney nodded. "I took you in because you were sick and your aunt was too busy to take care of you. You seem to think I'm keeping you here against your will. I'm not."

Lily looked at the clock next to her bed. It was noon. In twelve hours she was supposed to meet Clark outside. Mrs. Gurney said she could leave now, but would she change her mind in twelve hours? Lily didn't know what to do. She sat down on the bed and rubbed her cheek. Mrs. Gurney stood over her. She took Lily's hand away from her face. "Lily, are you all right? Your face just then. You looked . . . vacant."

Lily heard the distant sound of thunder. Clouds darkened the colors of the stained glass window. "Do you really hope that your son will return after all these years?" The question came out of Lily's mouth unbidden. It was the last thing she had expected to say. She stared at the open door, wondering why she didn't just run out of it. Instead, she stayed where she was, perched on the edge of the bed.

Mrs. Gurney's face grew almost soft. "What a strange question. It is my choice for him to return. I made the choice to believe that he would not leave me. And it is a choice that I have never regretted. Are you ready to leave now?" Mrs. Gurney asked gently.

Lily thought about Clark. She would make a choice *for* him. She would make the choice to wait to see him tonight. "My aunt comes back tomorrow," said Lily. "By then, I'll be ready to go home."

"I think so too," said Mrs. Gurney. "If you don't mind, I'll paint a little. I just need a fresh glass of water."

Lily could guess what would be in that fresh glass of water. Mrs. Gurney left the room, leaving the door wide open. Lily looked out the door at the hallway. She could see the banister leading down to the living room.

In a few minutes, Mrs. Gurney returned, carrying her glass. She sat down at the easel. She went to work on the painting. Lily ate yogurt and fresh fruit, but only pretended to sip the tea. Every once in a while, she went into the bathroom and emptied her mug into the toilet. Everything else might be shadowy—but there was one reality she could hang on to. Ever since she had stopped drinking the tea, she had felt stronger.

The storm outside never seemed to get closer. The room felt stuffy. "Do you mind if I open the window?" she asked.

"Of course not," said Mrs. Gurney.

Lily went to the window. The nails were gone. She stared at the window, puzzled. Had this been another hallucination? Had she dreamed that the window had been nailed shut? But she did have that scratch on her arm. The window slid up easily. She looked down at the bed. The wind was blowing at least fifteen miles an hour, yet the sheets remained unruffled. She couldn't find Clark. What if he had been toying with her and wouldn't show up? Lily got dizzy looking down at the bed. She worried that she was going to throw up. She swayed.

Mrs. Gurney gently led her away from the window. Lily allowed herself to be guided back to bed, like a child. Mrs. Gurney tucked her in and then went back to her painting. Lily lay on the bed.

She squinted as she tried to focus on the roses on the wallpaper. The painted thorns looked as big and as thick as a boy's finger. They were growing before her eyes. She shuddered, trying to make the hallucination go away.

Mrs. Gurney stretched her torso away from the easel to get a better perspective. She stood up, taking a sip of her drink. "I think my painting's finished. I'll take it with me. The paint fumes might be bothering you." She picked up the painting and her glass and headed toward the door.

"May I see my portrait?" Lily asked her.

"Perhaps later," said Mrs. Gurney. "It will be something for you to look forward to. I need to let it sit."

"Why can't I see it now?" Lily insisted.

"Instant gratification is really no gratification," said Mrs. Gurney. She paused. "By the way, Lily, I have to go out this evening. I'll be out rather late. I hope you don't mind. You do seem better, although I think you're having a little spell now. But still your color is fresher. I think you'll be fine on your own. Is that all right with you?"

"Yes!" Lily nearly shouted. An electric current coursed through Lily's body. She clamped her mouth shut, fearful that if she opened her mouth she would sob in relief. Mrs. Gurney was leaving the house. It would be easy to escape and meet Clark.

"Lily? Are you sure you'll be all right?"

Lily managed to nod, staring at the wallpaper. The thorns were growing in front of her eyes. They were now bigger—bigger than a boy's arm, and they curled in on one another in a horrible way.

Lily closed her eyes, but when she opened them again the thorns were still there. She had stopped drinking the tea. She had thought that the tea was to blame for everything. But if it was only the tea, why was she now having hallucinations worse than ever before? Lily had no answers. But Mrs. Gurney was going out and Clark had promised her that they would be together. She could hold on until the evening.

CLARK COULD SEE A FEW STARS TWINKLING, ALTHOUGH HE REMEMBERED FROM HIGH SCHOOL SCIENCE THAT STARS DIDN'T TWINKLE. The effect of the light traveling through the earth's atmosphere created an illusion. The stars peeked through the clouds, like millions of eyes watching in a movie theater.

In space, there was no twinkle. In space there was just steady, never-ending light. Not exactly never ending, Clark realized. Even stars died. It just took them billions and billions of years, but they died.

Clark stood with his elbows on the railing of the Boardwalk and looked down at the outline of the bed on the lawn. With one fluid motion, he vaulted the railing and landed on the soft grass. He walked to the bed. It had started to drizzle lightly but the clouds were still so thin, the moon and the stars shone through.

Clark's hair whipped around his face. He went to the spotlight, and using the end of his T-shirt, he unscrewed the light, just the way Lily had. It seemed like years since Lily had sat on the bed, the strange mesmerized expression on her face. Clark could have tried to save her then, but he hadn't. He had been selfish. He wouldn't be selfish again.

Lily had wanted darkness. Now he needed the dark. He had never been afraid of the dark. It always had been a good place to hide. But he could never trust the darkness to last. His mother always found him at dawn. He reached out a hand and touched the bed. It was bone-dry, but the sheets started to crumble with his touch. It was like the shivers of brittle dust from a broken fine china plate. He needed to lie down on the brittle sheet. The bed was a magnet. "It's a choice," he had told Lily. He smoothed out the blanket, like a child, making the bed just so. He lifted his head and looked at the stained glass window. Tears ran down his cheeks. He lay down on the bed and waited.

Lily listened for sounds in the house. Every nerve was on alert. A while ago, Mrs. Gurney had looked in on her, and Lily had pretended to be asleep. Then she had closed the door. Lily had heard the front door open and close. She couldn't really believe she was alone. Lily had waited, staring at the numbers on her watch as they clicked forward. The house was silent.

Finally her watch said 11:52. It was time to go. She swung her legs to the side of the bed and forced herself to get up. The thorns on the wallpaper looked as thick as a boy's thigh. Lily bit down on her lip hard. When Clark had brought her into the room, he had made a joke about there being no thorns. He had tried to prove to her that the thorns were just painted.

Lily reached out and touched the wallpaper the way Clark had. She jumped. Something pricked her finger.

A nail's pointed end faced out. Lily put her finger in her mouth. Her own blood tasted warm and salty.

She forced herself to take a deep breath. Even though she hadn't drunk any tea for twenty-four hours, it must still be in her system. Something in the tea was causing her to see things that weren't there.

She looked down at herself. The roses on her nightgown were growing thorns too. She flung the nightgown over her head and stood by the side of the bed.

She went to the closet, desperate to find her own clothes. She opened the closet door. The only things hanging in the closet were the dozens of perfectly pressed and matched nightgowns with roses. Terrified, Lily slammed the closet door shut. She leaned against the door feeling as if the thorns were going to grow and impale her, like a medieval torture device. Her legs were trembling. She staggered to the bureau drawer. She found a pair of boy's baggy swimming trunks in an ugly blue color. They must have belonged to Mrs. Gurney's son. Lily didn't care. At least they had no roses on them. She put them on. They felt wonderfully soft to the touch, and reassuringly real. Stuffed in a corner of a drawer, she found a plain gray T-shirt. It smelled musty. She pulled it on anyway. Her hands were like icicles. She rubbed her hands on her thighs to warm them.

She went to the door of the bedroom and put her ear against the wood. The wood felt satiny, almost soft. Lily listened at the door. Somewhere down the hall a board creaked. Lily froze. Could Mrs. Gurney have returned? Was she in the house? Lily stood like a statue. There was no other sound.

She opened the door and stepped around the doorway into the hall. The hallway was dark, and there was no light coming from downstairs. In fact, the only light in the entire house seemed to be from Lily's bedroom.

Suddenly the lights behind her in the bedroom went out! Plunged into total darkness, Lily's heart raced. Her armpits, her palms, even the V's between her fingers began to sweat with terror, even though Lily hadn't been scared of the dark for years.

When she was only three, her father had given her a night-light, shaped like a unicorn. After he died, she had told herself that only babies were afraid of the dark, and she had given the unicorn to her mother. Her mother had urged her to keep it, but Lily refused. The unicorn still shone in her mother's bedroom, but Lily had always been proud of the fact that she didn't need a night-light.

Now the darkness terrified her. She knew that her life was in the balance. If she did not escape from the darkness of this house, she could die. She forced herself to move forward. She rounded a corner of the hall. She continued moving, down the hall toward the stairs, using the wall against the back of her hand as her guide. She struggled with her fear, knowing that terror could kill her. Her mother, Bonnie, Reggie, Aunt Andrea, even Clark—they all belonged to an

alternate universe. The only thing real was this
house—this darkness and this terror.

She tiptoed down the stairs. She tried to tell herself that the light going off in the bedroom was just
a power outage. They happened often in Atlantic City
during storms. She reached the bottom of the stairs.
A light shone from beyond the archway of the foyer
in the living room. The house wasn't blacked out. If
there was no power blackout, who could have turned
off the light in her bedroom? She waited, listening for
sounds, but there was only silence. Was somebody
hiding in the living room? What if Mrs. Gurney had
not gone out and it was a trap?

She could retreat back to the bedroom, but in the
bedroom, the thorns were waiting for her, growing.
She knew she would go mad if she returned to the
bedroom. Outside, Clark had promised her that he
would help her escape.

In order to get outside, she had to cross the
threshold of the living room. She tried to peer into
the living room. The heavy drapes were drawn across
the glass windows, blocking out the light from the
moon and the stars. The room seemed empty. The
only light was a small beam aimed down at the
middle of the room, a tiny spotlight above a painting.
She tried to step across the archway toward the front
door and freedom.

As if being sucked in by a giant magnet, her feet
turned into the living room. Her eyes locked on to
the painting. Lily grabbed the frame of the arch to the

living room and tried to resist, but her body was not
her own to control. Some force pushed her toward
the painting, the finished portrait of herself.

In the painting, Lily was surrounded by black
waves, but her face was bathed in pure white light.
She looked dead. Lily trembled. She heard a voice
inside her head scream, "Run away!" The words gave
her strength. She pulled herself away from the painting. With her first step, the spotlight above the painting clicked off. Lily heard someone breathing in the
corner.

Paralyzed by the darkness, Lily knew that someone
was in the room with her. She wanted to run, but she
couldn't. She fell forward to her hands and knees,
curling into a ball to make herself smaller. She held
her breath and waited. She heard someone inhale.
Whoever had turned the light off was definitely in the
room with her now. Lily's fingers fumbled on the
bottom shelves of a bookcase.

Suddenly every light in the living room blazed on.
Lily screamed. Mrs. Gurney sat on a couch, dressed in
a white terry cloth beach robe. Her gray hair was
down, flowing to her shoulders, like a young girl's.
She held a remote control device in her hand.
Obviously she had been using it to control the lights.
"Lily," she said calmly. "What are you doing on the
floor?"

Lily couldn't breathe. She grabbed a book, as if it
were a weapon.

"Lily?" repeated Mrs. Gurney. She stood up and

walked over to the portrait of Lily and studied it, almost critically. Then she took six steps and stood over the real Lily. She reached out a hand. "Let me help you up."

Lily shook her head stubbornly. She grasped a shelf of the bookcase and pulled herself up. She was taller than Mrs. Gurney, and the book was in her right hand. It was heavy, bound in blue-green leather with gold lettering. The book was heavy enough to bash down on Mrs. Gurney's head. With both hands, Lily raised the book over her head.

Mrs. Gurney smiled at her, not in the least afraid. That smile was more terrifying than anything Lily had experienced. Mrs. Gurney shook her head, like a mother reprimanding a child. "Give me the book," she said gently.

Lily shook her head, sobbing. Mrs. Gurney smiled again, as if Lily were a toddler having a tantrum. Suddenly Lily melted to the floor into a little ball. Mrs. Gurney pried the book out of her hand. "There, that's better," she said. Lily stayed in a fetal position, her long legs drawn up to her belly, her head buried in her chest.

"You are such a silly child," said Mrs. Gurney in a singsong voice. She reached down and tugged on Lily's arm. Lily tried to keep herself in a tight ball, but with no more effort than a mother picking up an infant, Mrs. Gurney pulled Lily to her feet. Lily struggled feebly, but Mrs. Gurney just laughed. She dragged Lily over to the couch.

"I think you'll be more comfortable here than on

the floor." Mrs. Gurney's bony freckled breastplate peeked out from the collar of the robe. "Sit down, dear," she said, her voice more insistent. She jerked at Lily's hand and Lily sank into the cushions, just as she had that first day when she had brought her tour to this house. It seemed so long ago. "Didn't you feel foolish on the floor?"

To her horror, Lily's head bobbed up and down, nodding in agreement.

Mrs. Gurney patted her knee reassuringly. She still had the book that Lily had tried to kill her with in her hand. Mrs. Gurney looked at the spine of the book and read the title out loud. "*The Sea* by Robert Miller."

Lily's hand went up to her mouth. She gagged. She wanted to put her thumb in her mouth like a little girl. She fought against the urge to suck her thumb, knowing that if she did so, it would be another victory for Mrs. Gurney. She clamped her hand between her legs.

Mrs. Gurney gave her an amused smile. "That's not very ladylike, dear," she said. She laughed. "But it is your choice."

Lily shuddered at the word *choice*. She had no choice—that was the terror. Her body was numb. She was incapable of moving. Mrs. Gurney ignored Lily's trembling. "How odd you chose this book. It was one of my son's favorite books. Do you know it?"

Lily shook her head dumbly. She had grabbed it randomly.

"I think we should go down to the sea, you and I,"

said Mrs. Gurney abrubtly. She stood up, wrapping the robe around her tighter. "Come on, Lily. You were trying to leave, weren't you?"

Lily's mouth opened. "YES!" she screamed, so loud she thought the windows would shatter.

"You don't need to shout, my dear. I can hear you. I will accompany you just to the water's edge."

From deep within Lily came a bellow. "NO!"

"Ah, but I must insist," said Mrs. Gurney, as if they were having a polite conversation. She took Lily's hand in hers.

"Please no," sobbed Lily. She tried to sink down into the cabbage roses of the couch's pillow, but something pricked her, like the deep thorn of a rose. She jumped up. She stuck her hand in the pocket of her shorts. She felt something balled up in there. She pulled it out. It was Clark's handkerchief, but the strange Gothic lettering had changed. Lily could see the word "Gurney" embroidered clearly. The handkerchief was just another of Mrs. Gurney's tricks. She threw the handkerchief away, thrusting her arm out.

"You and I are going for a walk," said Mrs. Gurney, taking advantage of the moment and grabbing Lily's arm. She took Lily's hand like a child.

26

MRS. GURNEY OPENED THE FRONT DOOR. It had been days since Lily had felt cool air against her face. The air felt good and real; Lily gulped at it. For an instant, she had a prayer that Mrs. Gurney's power over her would be broken. Mrs. Gurney stood at her side, patiently allowing Lily to breathe in and out. In the moonlight, Mrs. Gurney looked incredibly beautiful, ageless, like a goddess.

"Come, Lily," said Mrs. Gurney. Lily's bare toes dug into the grass of the lawn, but it was as if the lawn had turned into sticklers, pricking her, forcing her forward.

Clark saw the front door open from the bed. He rolled over on his stomach, like a kid watching television. He watched as Lily and Mrs. Gurney moved closer. It was all happening as he hoped.

Mrs. Gurney walked carefully along the lawn, her own bare feet skimming the grass, obviously not bothered by any pain. She kept her hand in Lily's. She led Lily across the lawn to the bed. "Hmmm, the spotlight must have burned out. I'll have to remember to replace it."

They got closer to the bed. Lily thought she saw a lump in the middle. She pointed. "No, no," said Mrs.

Gurney, again scolding Lily like a child. "This isn't time for your nap. First you must come for a swim."

"I don't know how to swim," Lily managed to gasp out.

"Yes, it's a beautiful night for a swim," said Mrs. Gurney, pretending to misunderstand.

Clark rolled off the bed, hiding under it. He couldn't let either of them see him yet.

Lily wanted to lie down on the bed. A wave of exhaustion hit her. She sank to her knees on the grass by the bed. Clark could almost touch her bare leg.

Mrs. Gurney yanked on her arm twice. With each tug, shocks of pain shot through Lily's knees. Lily lurched. She bounced to her feet, as if she were on one end of a bungee chord.

Lily didn't want to die in the water. In one desperate move, she grabbed the knob on the drowned boy's headboard. She felt that her only hope was to hold on to the bed. She gripped it with all her might. Mrs. Gurney raised her free hand. She slapped Lily across the face so hard that Lily bit down on her tongue. Lily shrunk back in pain, but she did not let go of the bedpost.

"You bitch!" yelled Mrs. Gurney, her nursery school manner gone. Lily licked the blood from the edge of her mouth, feeling a surge of power. If Mrs. Gurney was angry with her, then she had a chance. If only she could hold on to the bed, she would be safe.

Mrs. Gurney raised her hand to hit her again. Instinctively, Lily ducked her head to avoid the blow, and put her hands up to protect herself.

Mrs. Gurney laughed triumphantly. Lily had let go of the bed.

Hidden under the bed, Clark had heard the slap, and he recoiled, as if the hand had hit his face. He bit down on his tongue, tasting blood. It might be the last time he would ever bleed.

"Enough of that," said Mrs. Gurney. She gripped Lily's wrist. Her grip was like an iron band. Thorns pricked at Lily, thrusting her forward toward the sea. Sobbing, Lily couldn't resist.

The lawn gave way to sand. Mrs. Gurney forced Lily to walk under the Boardwalk. Almost daintily, Mrs. Gurney picked her way among the empty pizza boxes and garbage. Her grip never loosened on Lily's wrist.

The sand was cold and damp. Lily's feet sank. She stumbled. Mrs. Gurney caught her. Her gray hair whipped around her face. The waves were louder now.

Only when the water was lapping at their toes did Mrs. Gurney let go of Lily's wrist. "Now don't you go in without me," warned Mrs. Gurney. She giggled. Lily could not move. It was as if iron chains encircled her chest, tying her arms to her side. The chains might be invisible, but they felt real and painful and they dug into Lily's flesh, rooting her to where she stood with her feet in the water.

The water was warm, warmer than the night air. Mrs. Gurney looked at Lily, as if making sure that the chains were secure. Then she undid the tie of her robe and dropped it from her shoulders.

Naked, her breasts hung down, flattened and thin with age. But her legs were like a young girl's. Lily tried to turn her head away, but it was as if an iron collar was around her neck forcing her to look only at Mrs. Gurney.

Mrs. Gurney laughed. "Don't be a prude. I always loved to swim in the nude." She giggled. "I just made up a poem, didn't I? Prude and nude rhyme."

She laughed.

Lily's chin was high, forced up by the feel of iron biting into her neck. "Let me go," she begged.

"Oh, I can't," said Mrs. Gurney. She took a step toward Lily, her body gleaming in the moonlight. She touched Lily's hand and it was as if the chains dropped from Lily's body.

Lily gasped for air. "Now it's time for us to go for a swim," said Mrs. Gurney. "It's hard to swim with chains on, isn't it? One would drown." Mrs. Gurney laughed again.

Lily's mind was racing. Lily had been sure the chains had been in her imagination, but Mrs. Gurney spoke about them as if they were real. What was real? She had no freedom left. No choices. She was under Mrs. Gurney's spell and nothing and nobody could save her. Not even Clark. He wasn't here. Perhaps he had never planned on helping her—it had just been one last game that he wanted to play.

Mrs. Gurney gave her a funny look. "I just remembered," she said in a perfectly normal voice. "You don't swim, do you? Ah well, you don't have to," said

Mrs. Gurney. "You just have to hold on to me."

"No!" screamed Lily. The sand encased her feet, as if it were cement. She could not move. Mrs. Gurney took a step toward her. She grabbed Lily's wrist again and slowly pulled Lily into the water.

Now instead of being bound by iron chains, seaweed twisted itself around Lily's body, binding her legs together. With little hops the buoyant salt water lifted Mrs. Gurney on her toes and with each step, Lily was dragged in deeper. The water inched up higher and higher, first on her thighs, then her waist, then her breasts.

Salt from Lily's tears mingled with the salt of the ocean. Mrs. Gurney was shorter than Lily, and the water soon reached up to her neck. Her gray hair floated onto Lily's shoulder. Lily trembled. She could see the bright lights of the casinos above the Boardwalk, but they seemed as far away as the light of Mars or Jupiter.

A wave broke over Lily's head. She swallowed salt water and started to gag. Mrs. Gurney was at her side, floating on her back. "It can be peaceful," she said, kicking her toes playfully. Phosphorescent plankton glowed with each kick.

Lily's head went under the waves again. She sputtered for air. She was going to die. She felt something grip her leg. She knew it would be an iron manacle, chaining her ankles together, dragging her to the ocean floor.

She kicked out furiously, managing to break away for a second.

She felt Mrs. Gurney's hands on her shoulders, pushing her under the water. Suddenly other hands grabbed at her from behind.

Warm arms grabbed at her. On a crest of a wave, Clark's face popped in front of Lily's eyes. Was he to be the last face she imagined before she died?

Clark's arms grabbed her across the chest like a lifesaver and he kicked toward shore. "Just float. I've got you!" So this was the peace before one died, Lily thought. Her mother had always promised her that at the very end, her father had not known fear or pain. Lily hadn't known whether to believe her or not, but she allowed herself to float in Clark's imaginary arms—sure that this was the end. Her mother was right. It was peaceful.

"Don't struggle," Clark said, spitting out salt water.

Lily lay on her back. His voice sounded so real. The last thing she wanted to do was to struggle. Clark needn't have worried. Was she dead yet? She was fearful that at any moment Mrs. Gurney would manage to snatch her out of Clark's arms.

A wave broke over Lily's head. She sputtered. "It's okay. We're almost there," said Clark.

Lily felt him stand up, his head above the water. He helped her stand. Lily shook herself. She was alive, not dead. She was standing on sand. She was almost breathless with joy. "You're real!" she gasped.

"You're safe," Clark whispered. With his arm around her waist, he half carried her to the shore.

27

CLARK HELD HER, BUT HE KEPT HIS FACE TURNED
TOWARD THE SEA. The tide was coming up, and the
waves ebbed and flowed at their legs. He thought of
moving Lily farther up the beach, but she seemed
rooted to the spot. He held her tighter.

"Mrs. Gurney! Mrs. Gurney! She's out there!"
moaned Lily.

"Hush, hush!" whispered Clark.

"You've got to believe me," repeated Lily. "She
wanted me to drown like her son. And I followed her.
I had iron chains around me."

"Like all the others that drowned here," said Clark.

Lily looked up at him. His face was covered with
sand. She wiped a few grains of sand away from his
eyes. "I stopped drinking the tea, but it must have a
residual effect. Tonight, it was as if she had me spellbound. I couldn't resist. I let her lead me to the sea
like a cow to the slaughterhouse."

"Lily, you're safe," said Clark.

Lily shook her head. "I'm not safe. She'll come
back. She'll do it again. If not to me, to some other
kid next summer. We've got to stop her."

Clark smiled down at her. "The White Knight," he
said.

"What?"

"It's like playing my mother at chess. You'll never win. You want to be the White Knight, but it's her chess game."

Lily wasn't listening to him. "Mrs. Gurney. She's a maniac. And she has some power. I don't understand it, but . . . " She stared out at the ocean, sure that Mrs. Gurney would come back for her. Clark tilted her face toward his. "Stop talking about her," he said fiercely. "Forget her." Lily tried to shake her head, but Clark held her chin in his hand firmly. He kissed her. Her mind registered panic because she was responding—here at this moment when just seconds ago she had been sure she was dying, she felt a thudding excitement.

Clark's tongue searched her mouth, as if he knew that this was the only way to keep her from talking, from thinking, to shut her up. He kept his mouth glued to hers. He lifted his mouth from her lips. She started to say something, and he kissed her again. He wouldn't let her talk. Her lips opened. His hands roamed up and down her back, warming her. He wanted this sensation to be the last he remembered.

Lily opened her eyes. She wanted to see him. Her hands went around him, feeling the strong muscles of his back. She pressed him closer to her. Finally Clark took his mouth off hers, knowing they both needed to come up for air. He kept his eyes on her. Lily turned her head a fraction of an inch.

She screamed! Mrs. Gurney rose out of the water, luminous plankton gleaming on her shoulders and breasts.

Naked, she stood over them. "That's enough, son," she said. "Bring her in."

CLARK FELL BACK ON THE SAND AS IF SHOT. His hands were still around Lily's back and she fell on top of him. "I could have made it easy on her," said Mrs. Gurney. "It could have been peaceful. But no, you didn't want it that way." She laughed.

"Bitch!" spat out Clark, his mouth full of sand.

Lily struggled to her feet, but Clark's arms pinned her down. "Bitch!" Clark screamed again.

"Then as you have told me many times, that makes you a son of a bitch," said Mrs. Gurney calmly. "You're very funny. I saw you watching, like a lump in your bed. And then you hid under the bed while I had to slap her. Very amusing, Clark."

"Your bed!" sputtered Lily.

"I think your girlfriend is confused. Poor thing. She thought you were rescuing her. Now it will be so much more painful having to go through it all again."

Mrs. Gurney walked over to her robe although she didn't seem to be the slightest bit embarrassed to be naked in front of Clark. She put on her robe, tying the sash tight around her waist. "All right, Clark, have it your way. You take her into the sea."

"Clark, no!" howled Lily. She tried to stand and

run away, but Mrs. Gurney pointed a finger at her, and iron chains bit into her arms and legs. But this time it was not only the chains. Thorns dug into her like a thousand needles.

Mrs. Gurney had been right. Like a sadistic torturer returning to his or her victim, it *was* so much worse the second time. Clark ignored Lily, ignored her pain. Nothing in the world existed for him except the gray-haired woman, mocking him.

"Tell her, Clark," said Mrs. Gurney. "She's special to you, isn't she? So let her be the one who knows the truth before she drowns."

"Shut up, Mother! Just shut up!" screamed Clark.

Lily's knees buckled with the weight of the chains. She sank into the sand. Her lips were still swollen from Clark's kisses. She dropped her head into the sand.

Mrs. Gurney went to her and took her chin in her hand. Lily flopped like a whale impaled on a harpoon. Mrs. Gurney's robe flew in the breeze. "My son," she said simply. "Every summer, he comes back to me. Just as I told you, but you didn't believe me. He comes back to his bed. I couldn't bear to lose him, you see."

"It's her fault," said Clark, spitting his words into the wind. "She won't let me die. She was drinking one night—and she wanted me to swim with her. She disgusted me. I swam farther and farther out!"

"I screamed at him to come back," yelled Mrs. Gurney. "I screamed and screamed until I was hoarse. I thought I lost him forever. I was beside myself with grief. I put the bed out—not even knowing then that there was hope. And then young Jimmy Cannon, I took him swimming, and he drowned, and Clark woke up on the bed. What a miracle! I discovered that every summer if I sacrificed someone, Clark could come back."

"A miracle," mocked Clark. "Come, Lily." Clark grabbed her arm. His hand was as cold as the imaginary iron binding her. He forced her to stand. He looked deep into her eyes. "It's time to go back into the sea," he said.

Lily struggled. The chains cut into her. A manacle gripped her neck. It was Clark's hand on the back of her neck, forcing her into the sea. "You bastard, no!" Lily shouted. This time she was not hypnotized like before. This time she had her strength back. She dug her heels into the sand and pulled away from him, but Clark was as strong as she. His hand was around her waist. It was a struggle of equals.

Suddenly she felt no supernatural chains, no thorns, no seaweed binding her, but inch by inch Clark pulled her toward the water.

She took her fist and pummeled him. He flinched, but he didn't let go of his grip. "Don't do it, you bastard! Don't! Clark, let me go!"

"Mom, help me. She's strong!" he yelled.

Mrs. Gurney grinned. Her teeth glowed in the moonlight. She shook off her robe and practically skipped into the water, like a child. She grabbed Lily's free arm. Lily twisted and turned, but the grips on her arms just grew tighter. Together, mother and son dragged her into the waves.

Lily kicked and thrashed, but they pulled her in deeper and deeper. She felt herself sucked and clutched by the currents. A wave knocked her backward. She gagged, swallowing salt water, but each held on to a hand so Lily couldn't break free and push to the surface. Another wave broke over her head. She came up and gulped air into her starved lungs with a whooping roar. The force of the wave caused Clark to lose his grip on her. Mrs. Gurney held on tighter than before. She dived down under the waves, dragging Lily with her. Lily couldn't hold her breath any longer. She started to black out. A karate chop bore down on her left wrist. Lily felt the vibration under the water. Mrs. Gurney let go.

Something or someone pushed her toward the surface. Her head broke into the air, just as another wave pummeled her. Lily felt somebody push her toward shore. "Lily, go!" screamed Clark. "I had to bring you back in so I could get her out here! Swim for the shore!"

"I can't swim!" screamed Lily. Mrs. Gurney's hands were reaching out for her.

"Do it!" Clark shouted. "You can! You must save yourself. I'll take care of her." Clark twisted in the water and faced his mother. He leaped half out of water, riding a wave. His torso gleamed with luminous light.

"Let go!" he thundered. For a moment he rode the

top of the wave like an ancient god. Then he pounced down on his mother and held her head under the water.

Lily screamed and tried to swim toward shore. A surge of water lifted her like a piece of driftwood and tumbled her into a hollow in the sand. The retreating wave all but floated her out again. But somehow, her arms pulled at the water. She kicked. She was swimming. It was more pathetic than any dog paddle, but she was swimming. With each stroke, she got closer to the shore.

Lily felt sand under her feet. Another retreating wave grabbed at her. Almost too late, she thrust out her arms and dug into the soft sand. On her hands and knees she crawled toward the beach. She turned and faced the sea. Clark's face was bobbing in the water beyond the breaker. His skin was nearly translucent. It was covered with phosphorescence. He gave off a ghostly glow.

His head disappeared under a wave. Lily stood up, trying to see him. She felt something drag on her leg. She screamed, thinking that it was Mrs. Gurney, resurrected again. But it was just a piece of seaweed touching her calf.

Lily sank facedown in the sand, her feet still in the water. She lay like that until dawn.

LILY LOOKED DOWN AT HER ARMS. The salt from the ocean had dried and crusted in little curlicues, echoing the edges of the sea. She had sand in her hair and ears and in the creases near her eyes. The sweet light of the dawn lit the ocean with a pinkish, almost girlish, tone. Lily couldn't believe she was among the living. She looked out at the ocean, seeing Clark's face disappearing again and again below the black waves.

At first he must have thought that she was the perfect victim for his mother. He must have thought because she was excited and intrigued by the supernatural that she would fit into his mother's house as naturally as one of her paintings. He might have even thought that she would have wanted to die to be with him. But then Clark had come to love her. Lily was like no other. She helped free him from his mother—at last. He had forced his mother to finally let him go, but to do that he had to let Lily go too.

Tears rolled down her cheeks. She wiped them away. She stood up. The muscles along her shoulder blades ached. She swung her arms, trying to loosen them, and then she remembered. Her muscles ached because she had swum. Clark had left her with a gift.

She had saved herself. She could swim. She walked up the steps to the Boardwalk.

People passed her, without a second glance, as if she was just another teenager who happened to have gone swimming at dawn in shorts and a T-shirt instead of a bathing suit. She felt incredibly grubby. She stopped in front of the public showers and went inside. She didn't even realize that it was the same shower from which Clark had called her.

On the women's side, she stepped into the shower. There was no hot water, but the cool, fresh water washed the salt away. She stood under the shower's blast, lifting her chin to the water—letting it run down her, not even bothering to take off the T-shirt and shorts she had found in the drawer in Clark's room. She got out of the shower. She half dried herself off with an abandoned towel.

When she stepped outside, gray clouds had rolled in from the ocean. A thin wet drizzle had begun. Lily walked along the Boardwalk, feeling dazed. She passed the fortune-teller's shop.

The girl Marie stood outside of her shop. "Are you all right?" she asked.

Lily nodded. She thought about the tenth card at the reading. The Hanged Man. The card of sacrifice and surrender. Clark had taught her much about them both. Until he had met Lily, he had surrendered to his mother. He had allowed his mother to sacrifice a living teenager, so he, a dead one, could come back, year after year, just for the summer. But in the end, he had sacrificed himself so that she should live, and so that his mad existence would finally end.

"Do you want to come in and get dry?" Marie asked.

Lily shook her head.

"Please," begged Marie. "I won't charge you."

Lily blinked. "It's raining," she managed to croak out. They were the first words she had spoken since she had almost drowned.

"Yes," whispered Marie. "That's why you should come in and get dry."

Lily shook her head. "If it's raining, then . . . "

"Then what?" asked Marie.

"Nothing," said Lily. She hurried away, back in the direction from which she had come—back to Mrs. Gurney's house.

"Wait . . . ," shouted Marie.

Lily ignored her. She would have to see for herself. She started to run along the Boardwalk. The drizzle was more persistent, wetting her through with surprising efficiency. Tourists hurried past her, anxious to get out of the rain—but Lily ran on, determined to see for herself.

The rosebushes were blowing in the soft wind, but the buds looked brown and withered. Lily hesitated in front of Mrs. Gurney's house. The bed looked so small. She vaulted over the railing, and stood on the lawn. She looked down on the bed. The pillows and the blanket and the sheets were soaked with rain. The bed was wet. Mrs. Gurney had told her the bed stayed dry, because every summer when Clark returned, he was cold and wet. Clark would never return again.

Lily stepped on the soft rain-soaked ground. She looked down. Something was growing under the bed. She looked at the lawn. Lilies of the valley were blooming everywhere, and the roses were dying. The curse was broken. It was a final gift from Clark.

Suddenly Lily heard someone call her from the door of the house. She jumped back. Dr. Kemika waved to her. He came across the lawn. Lily got ready to run.

"I was looking for you," he said. "Mrs. Gurney is missing. They found her robe down on the beach. Did you see her last night? She was supposed to come to a benefit for the hospital, but she never showed up."

Lily shook her head dumbly.

"I thought she might have talked to you last night. She left a package in the living room with your name on it."

"She didn't," Lily blurted out.

Dr. Kemika looked at her strangely. "Oh yes, she did," he said. "You can come in and get it."

"I'm not stepping foot in that house again," Lily said. She waited for him to contradict her.

"Wait here," he said. "I'll bring it to you." He came out of the house, carrying a package wrapped in brown paper the size of a painting. "This had your name on it," he said.

Lily took it reluctantly.

"It could be valuable," said Dr. Kemika. "You should get it out of the rain."

Lily turned her back on him. He didn't try to stop

her. Lily wondered how much Dr. Kemika knew. Had Mrs. Gurney paid him to deceive her? She struggled with the painting as she walked down the wooden steps from the Boardwalk.

Underneath the boards, when she was alone, she tore the brown paper off the painting. It was Mrs. Gurney's portrait of Lily surrounded by black waves. Except her face had been painted over. Clark's face gazed out at her—looking almost translucent—the way he had the last time she had seen him.

Lily hadn't even realized she was crying. She wiped away her tears. The day she met Clark, he told her that he hated illusions. He would have hated this painting.

Lily picked it up. Farther up the beach, toward the casinos, some kids had built a bonfire. Flames spit in the drizzle, defying the rain.

Lily walked down the beach, carrying the painting. The kids were about her age.

"Hey" said one of the kids. "That's a beautiful painting. Can I have it?"

"No," said Lily. She put the painting into the flames. The fire licked at Clark's face. Lily stood over the fire until Clark's face disappeared the way it had in the ocean. She wouldn't need his mother's portrait to remember him. She would have his love. Empty-handed, she walked up the steps to the Boardwalk, and turned away from Mrs. Gurney's house, toward her aunt's apartment.